TERROR FROM ABOVE

Dick Enos

PublishAmerica
Baltimore

Hardcover 978-1-4560-7568-2
Softcover 978-1-4560-7569-9
PUBLISHED BY PUBLISHAMERICA, LLLP
www.publishamerica.com
Baltimore

Printed in the United States of America

Dedicated to my family who never stopped believing. And especially to the four girls who wouldn't let me give up and without whom none of this would have been possible. Shannon for her inspiration, Heather for keeping me headed in the right direction, Kathleen for the fixes (and cookies), and most of all my wife, Norma. Never once did she throw me under the bus. (Even though she wanted to a few times.)

PROLOGUE

The reports were coming in from everywhere. There was heavy flooding in the Midwest, earthquake damage on the West Coast, hurricane winds in the east. Almost reluctantly, the announcer picked up his copy and made his way to the broadcast booth. None of the news was good. It hadn't been for the last six weeks. Wearily he took his seat and nodded to the producer. The producer nodded back and started to count down with his fingers. When the fingers went away, the light came on. The announcer took a deep breath and began to read. "The strange weather across our nation continues to baffle the experts and pound away at the countryside. The torrential rains in the Midwest today gave way to a shower of hailstones bigger than softballs. The Cedar River has cut Cedar Rapids, Iowa, off from the rest of the world, making what's left of the town an island. Late this afternoon, twin tornadoes tore through the streets of Manhattan, taking lives, breaking windows, and hurtling cars about like toys." A copy boy entered the booth and handed him a sheet of teletype flimsy. His expression darkened as he read it. "This has just been handed to me… A typhoon has begun to build off the coast of California and is expected to make landfall in San Francisco later in the week. Everyone is being asked to prepare for the worst." He shook his head as though his listeners could see him. "Most of the Midwest has been declared a disaster area by the President. Little or no traffic is moving out of Chicago. He was asked earlier today how much more of this we can take, and he said, 'We will stand whatever terrors we must face! We are Americans! We will find a way to survive!'" But whatever that way was, it was not yet evident to the rest of the country. The announcer looked out of the booth at the blank, scared faces of his coworkers. There were no answers!

* * * * *

The night hung like a black shroud over the desert. To the far north lightning flashed in the sky, warning of the impending storm, and directly above, the clouds blotted out the moon, leaving only a faint glow in the sky.

That glow did little to enhance the shabby, brick building sticking up out of the desert sand. The faded sign on the side read "Gallagher Scientific Research," but if you'd come this far out into the desert, unless you were lost, you already knew that. It was a small research lab just big enough for a couple of electrical engineers and some lab help, never involved in anything bigger than a better toaster or maybe television. At this late hour only a few of the lights were on, and the only car in the lot was a beat-up, old station wagon with the same faded writing as the sign. A heavy chain-link fence protected the scrub brush from the evils of science. But the gates hung open, rusted in place, and the guard shack had been long since abandoned—or at least it appeared so, its windows empty of glass and door hanging askew. For a moment the clouds parted, and a shadow shifted inside. The shadow hesitated for a moment at the entrance to the shack, but then as the clouds rolled back together, it came alive and moved from concealment. As it did, it was revealed to be more than just a wraith in the night; it appeared to be a man. But if it was a man, he was unlike any this earth had ever seen. He was tall, almost inhumanly so, with long arms that reached nearly to his knees, a mop of dark-reddish hair crowning his long, triangular face. He was dressed like a villain in an old Western—dark suit, string tie. But he was no Wild West villain. When he moved, it was incredibly fast, his large, booted feet barely touching the ground. But his gait was awkward, disjointed, like his knees were too loose. In less than an instant, he was through the gate and across the small parking lot. When he reached the building, he spread himself so thin against the bricks that he nearly disappeared. His large ears pricked like those of an animal as he listened for the sounds of discovery. When none came, he began his mission once more.

From the side pocket of his jacket, he removed a small square of what looked like modeling clay. He pressed it into the side of the building, smoothing it into the rough cracks. Quickly he moved on, doing it three more times, once on each of the exterior walls. Finished, he flattened himself against the wall again. For a few, quick moments he watched the lighted windows and listened once again for sounds of discovery. When again none came, satisfied, he fled once more back across the lot and through the open gates. This time he didn't stop at the guard shack. He ran on out into the desert and dropped down behind a small hummock.

Crouched there, he pulled a device from his pocket. It was a small, square box the size of a pack of cigarettes. From the top he extended an antenna. Then, with a grin crossing his strange face, he pushed the single button on the device's surface. A tenth of a second later, the night was split by a giant whoosh followed by a roar, and the sun seemed to come up. Even behind his cover, the man was picked up and slammed against the ground. A wind tore at his clothes, and as the fireball that had been the lab rose into the night sky, the heat washed over him. Seconds after, he rose, dusted himself off, and with a nod at his handy work, loped off into the desert.

CHAPTER 1

I popped the canopy as I taxied in, letting the desert heat wash over me. The fading scream of my engine mixed with the cacophony of the air field. All around me other jets were constantly taking off and landing, with support vehicles flooding the field like ants servicing their masters. It was a circus compared to the quiet I'd just left behind. Since the weather crash, we were about the only place left flying, and it was up to us to report on conditions.

As I rolled to a halt, I unsnapped the buckles on my harness and stood up. I felt my knees pop as I did. I'd been cramped up way too long, but damn what a thrill! I leaned out and tossed my helmet down to my crew chief. I climbed out, and two steps across the wing and a short leap later, I was beside him. Joey and I had been together since Korea. "How was it up there, Captain?" There was a nasal twang to his voice that let you know right away he was native to California.

I shook my head. "Pretty rough. The air's getting about as choppy as the ocean. Don't know how much longer we'll be able to fly. The sample tanks are full, so make sure they get to the brain boys. I'm headed for Poncho's and that beer that Yeager owes me."

Joey scrunched up his face and shook his head. "'Fraid not, sir. The old man's been waiting. And he said to send you right over as soon as you came down. He even sent a car." He indicated to the jeep with a sweaty, bored corporal in it over by the mechanic's shed.

"Must be urgent then. The beer and Yeager will have to wait." I could feel the heat from the tarmac through my boots as I walked over to the jeep. As I climbed in, I said, "To HQ, and don't spare the horses. There's a cold beer waiting somewhere with 'Rick Steele' written on the side of it!" He tossed out his cigarette, and we roared across the compound.

The 412th Test Wing had moved onto the 300 thousand acres that was Edwards Air Force Base just after WWII to test jet airplanes, and I'd moved in with them. Then Korea heated up, and I went off to shoot down Russians. Now I was back, but instead of testing planes, I was running recon for the weather service. The base was expanding again and that meant a combination of brick buildings, tents, and Quonset huts were scattered between the hangers and the sheds. Flight Headquarters was one of the latter, with a big air conditioner stuck in one of the upper windows.

In a cloud of dust we slammed to a stop, and I rolled out of the jeep. I turned to thank the corporal, but the minute my feet hit the ground, he was gone like the Masked Man. I pushed open the door and stepped inside with half a grin. And then I felt it freeze on my face. It was like a refrigerator in there. I swore my lower jaw fell off as I said, "The colonel wanted to—"

A young lieutenant in a crisp, well-pressed uniform and a look of disdain he saved just for pilots cut me off before I could finish. "He's inside waiting. Said to go right in," and after a long pause he added, "sir."

Like a good little captain, I held my tongue. Some guys fly desks and hate the guys who don't. I walked on by and stepped into the inner office.

If it were possible, it was even colder in there. But when you saw the whale behind the desk, you knew why; he'd sweat at one of the poles. He shifted his bulk in his seat, and taking

10

the cigar stub from his mouth, he used it to motion me to the chair in front of his desk. "Sit down, Captain." The voice was old, tired gravel. And it seemed to come from somewhere around the side of his mouth rather than the center.

As I sat down, he hoisted himself from his chair, and I swear it groaned with release. He shuffled around the corner of his desk and walked over to the window that looked out onto the field. You could see the clouds roiling off to the west. "Pretty rough up there right now, I hear. Sometimes it makes me glad I'm grounded." His war record was legendary, but now it would take something as big as a transport to get him off the ground.

Normally I'd have let him reminisce, but I was thirsty and there was a free beer waiting. "You said it was urgent, sir?"

He clutched his hands behind his back as he came across the room. He winced with every step like his feet hurt. "Son, I've got some bad news…" He perched himself on the corner of the desk and laid a handful of sausages on my shoulder in what he thought was a gesture of concern. "There was an explosion last night at that lab where your brother worked, and he was killed."

Suddenly the ice that was freezing on my flight suit was on the inside of me. I'm sure I shivered. My last relative was gone. I pinched the bridge of my nose between my thumb and forefinger and shook my head to clear it. Maybe I didn't hear him right. "Did you say my brother Owen was killed last night, sir?"

He swiveled around on his enormous behind and picked up a telegram from the desk. He treated it like a snake that was going to bite him. "It came while you were upstairs. It's from the sheriff's office in that town where he lived. Says he was the only one there at the time."

That didn't surprise me. It was pretty much common knowledge that Owen liked to work alone and at night. A thousand questions flooded my mind, but I knew the answers weren't here. I scrubbed my hands over my face and said, "I'm going to need some time, sir."

"I expected that, Rick. Take as much as you need." As I rose from the chair, he gestured with his cigar again and said, "I got you a seat on the next transport headed that way. It leaves in two hours, so you'd better get a move on."

"Thank you, sir." I didn't even growl at the shavetale on the way out. When I stepped out into sunlight again, it had lost its warmth. Two hours later, a duffel bag stuffed with a few things I might need and I were in the back of a transport headed south.

As the engines droned outside, I took the first real time to think about my brother Owen. He and I were about as much alike as night and day. As a matter of fact, that's what Mom used to call us. He was born dark and brooding like Dad, and I was blonde and cheery. I was the risk-taker, invulnerable, the first to jump. Owen was steadfast and safe, planning every step. I went off to join the Air Corps, and he went off to college to become a scientist. When the war broke out I went overseas, and he went to a secret project in New Mexico. I shot down planes, he helped build *the bomb.*

When it was over, he stayed in New Mexico to help build better toasters, and I went right on chasing the sky. The folks died in a car accident just before Korea, and after that we hadn't been very close. He spent a lot of time spouting anti-government rhetoric and how he should never have helped build the bomb. Being part of that selfsame military-industrial complex, I got tired of being his whipping boy for what I do.

About three months ago, I got the first call from him since I'd been back. He seemed all upset—something about him

12

being in trouble with what he had learned, and that they were going to stop him. I had pretty much just shoved it into the file with rest of the crazy stuff he said. Now it turned out maybe this time he was right, and whoever "they" were had done just that. That was what I was on my way to find out.

The desert sun was just setting as we skidded to a stop on the runway. I thanked the crew, leaped out, and went looking for a rental car. An hour later I was in a 15-year-old, green Packard headed out of town again, a three-hour drive ahead of me.

CHAPTER 2

With the weather all out of whack, the weatherman had more airtime than the newsreaders. This time was no exception. He was back on the air again with a special bulletin. "Once more we are expecting massive amounts of rainfall. In some places it will amount to as much as three inches an hour, with wind gusts of over sixty miles per hour. The residents are being asked to go to the nearest designated shelter to wait out the storm. This is not a drill. The storm is rapidly approaching and will strike within the hour. Stay tuned for further updates." The red light went out, and he let out a heavy sigh. Turning to his producer, he asked, "How much longer are we going to be able to stay here?"

The producer, a thin man with a balding head, shrugged his shoulders inside his wrinkled jacket. "Don't know. Most everybody else is gone. The water's up over the curbs on the street. We may have to stay just because we can't get out. Not sure anybody's listening anymore, anyway. Power's out over most of the state." The weatherman lit a cigarette and settled into the chair to wait for his next bulletin. Whether or not anybody was listening, they'd keep broadcasting, just in case.

* * * * *

The town was bigger than I expected, running about 12 or 14 thousand people, and was kind of a combination of Old

West and New Modern. The sheriff's office was part of the Old Western: a single story, adobe-faced building with a wooden porch, two barred windows like eyes, and a wooden plank door in the middle of the wall. The lights were still on behind the windows, so I took for granted that justice never sleeps and pushed the door open.

The office was one big room with three desks, each corralled with a wooden fence and gate to stop them from roaming. In the center corral, an old cowboy in a tan-colored uniform was leaned back, reading a magazine with a half-naked woman being chased by aliens on the cover. At the sound of the door, he swung his feet to the floor and pushed up his cowboy hat with a rag. "Somethin' I can do for you, Major?"

"Actually, it's Captain, and I was looking for the sheriff," I said as I stepped inside the fence. He spit tobacco juice into an old coffee can and tossed down the book. With a grin that showed his teeth matched the brown in his mustache, he said, "Well then, this is your lucky day, 'cause you just found him. But if you've come to recruit me, you're not so lucky, 'cause I done my time back in the big one."

I forced a smile to my lips that I didn't feel, and I shook my head. "'Fraid not. I'm here to see about my brother." Then I proceeded to tell him who I was.

"Oh yeah, the science guy that blowed himself up. What can I do for ya?"

"Well, I'd kind of like to know what happened."

He bobbed his cowboy hat, spit in the can again, and slid open a drawer on his desk. From it he took a thin file, leafed through it, and pulled one paper out from the rest. Tossing the file on the desk, he waved the page like a flag and said, "Gas leak's what caused it all. From what was left, looked like it must have damn near filled the whole building before she blowed.

Doubt he was even awake to know what was happenin'. What with all the chemicals and science stuff in the building, it went up pretty much like one of them A-bombs you fellers are always droppin'. Must have been some fireball! Pretty much out by the time the fire department got there."

The look on my face must have tipped him off to what I was feeling, because he turned a bit red and looked down at the floor. "Sorry Major, wasn't thinkin'. But then I'm bettin' you seen worse in the war. Hell, probably caused worse."

I just let it all pass, because if I didn't, I was going to be in a cell for beating the hell out of the local law, and I didn't have that kind of time. "Was there anybody else around? What about a watchman or a guard?"

He shook his head, making his hat rock. He reached up and pulled it back snug. "Nope. They weren't doing nothin' out there that was secret enough somebody'd want to steal it."

"And who is 'they'?"

"The other couple of scientists—Gallagher and Hansen."

I knew I was wasting my breath, but I thought I'd ask anyway. "Have you talked to either one of them?"

He shook his head and spit again. "Didn't see much sense. It was all pretty much open and shut. Besides, they were both out of town."

They say that blood boils at 103.6 degrees centigrade, and mine was real close to it at that moment. "Do you mind if I go out and take a look around? I'd kind of like to see the last place he was alive." I hoped it didn't sound like I was laying it on too thick. From the look on his face, I wasn't.

"Don't see why not, but there's not much there but a big ol' hole. But I want you to know that if you get hurt, the county isn't responsible!"

I nodded to show him I understood and put my cap back on. "Has there been any kind of trouble before this?"

"Like I said, they weren't workin' on no secret projects."

I tried a long shot. "Do you know what they *were* working on?"

The cowboy hat rolled from side to side. "Nope."

I thanked him again and was about to step through the door when he called me back. "Where can I get in touch with you if I need to?"

"I'll be staying at my brother's. I've got to see about his stuff." As the door closed, I saw him reach for the phone.

* * * * *

As the door closed behind the captain, the sheriff picked up the phone and quickly dialed a number. There was a series of clicks on the other end, then a non-descript voice said, "Yes?"

"The brother just left. Said he was going out to the site in the morning. I don't think he believes me."

"Don't worry about it. It all will be taken care of." Then the phone went dead.

The sheriff hung up his end, swung his feet back onto the desk, and went back to reading his magazine.

* * * * *

I don't know why, but Owen's house surprised me. It was just your standard, Southwestern, low-slung, painted adobe with a tile roof. Maybe it was the fact that it was a house. Since Owen had left home, all he had lived in were various dorms where he'd worked.

I pulled the Packard into the driveway and shut it off. Then I sat in the seat for a few minutes more while I screwed up my courage enough to go inside. Yeah, I'd killed men, I'd watched friends die, but I was afraid of my brother's house. "Come on Rick, you telling me you're afraid of ghosts now?" I chided myself. And it seemed to break the spell. I pushed open the door and slid out of the car. I pulled my duffel bag from the back seat and set out for the front door. Long, slow, deliberate steps. I think I wanted it to take as long as possible to go the twenty feet or so. Then there I was, standing in front of his red-painted door. I lifted the rock on the stoop and there was the key, right where Mom and Dad always kept theirs. Old habits…

My first try was a fumble, and I dropped the key. The second time with only the slightest tremble, I scored. The door swung open, and I stepped inside of Owen's life.

The house smelled musty, sort of like the place where your Grandma lived. A smell that you can never really define—dying flowers, dust, and something I couldn't quite put my finger on. I shook my head, tried to grin, and flipped on the light. And I started! I dropped my duffel and was in a fighting stance before I realized that it was only the hall tree with Owen's coat and hat hanging on it. This time I did grin. I was turning into an old lady.

I picked my duffel bag back up and made my way to the back of the house, looking for the bedrooms. The first one I came to must have been Owen's. The bed was messed like he'd just crawled out, but that wasn't what caught my eye. It was the walls. They were covered with newspaper clippings. I clicked on the light for a better look. They were all about Korea, the H-bomb, civil unrest, HUAC, and the like. He'd always been an activist nut, but it looked like lately he was even more so. I don't think that surprised me. Owen was pretty much anti-government since the atomic bomb. But the other wall did leave me a bit wide-eyed. It was covered with clippings on

UFOs, from the first reports of the Roswell crash to almost daily sightings here in this part of New Mexico.

As I read the clippings, I noticed his desk cluttered with papers. Leafing through them, I began to wonder at the level of his sanity. There were notes on flying saucers and their directions of travel, strange propulsion units, weird devices, and sketches of half human-looking creatures. The few entries in his journal were even worse. "Nearly got caught today, getting closer, must work faster. Electromagnetism seems to be the key. Just need more control. Time is running out!!! Another test today at White Sands, it must be stopped!"

I closed the book and wiped my hand over my face, trying to wipe away the thoughts that filled my head. "What were you doing, Owen?" I whispered. "What were you *doing*?" I turned out the light and left the room to find the other bedroom. It had been a long day and I needed some sleep. As I turned down the bed, I pulled my service automatic from the shoulder holster under my fatigues and slid it under the pillow on the bed. Then I climbed out of my clothes and slumped down on the bed in my underwear. It couldn't have been more than a few minutes and I was sound asleep.

It was about three o'clock in the morning when I heard the sound of a window sliding open. As quietly as possible, I rolled off the bed and onto the floor, the .45 tight in my fist. For a long moment I lay listening to the sounds of the house, thinking that I might have imagined it. But then I heard the soft tread of someone, or something, coming down the hall. Quickly I pushed the pillows into a pile on the bed and covered them up. Then I padded silently over to the door.

I had just gotten behind it when the handle slowly began to turn. The only light was the dull glow of the street lights through the curtains. I sucked in a deep breath and hoped that whoever was in the hall couldn't hear the pounding of my heart. The door inched open, and the barrel of a silenced revolver poked in. It spit silently four times, each bullet making the covers on the bed jump.

Suddenly I started to tremble, and the steel seemed to have left my spine. As the pistol withdrew, I slid slowly to the floor in a puddle of sweat. It had been a long time since somebody had tried to kill me, and even then there was a jet under me to escape in. I sat there behind the door, listening to the sound of the footsteps as they receded, hoping that they wouldn't stop and come back. As I heard the sound of the window sliding shut, my breath returned in quick, short gasps. I squeezed my hand tight around the grip of the pistol, trying to take back control. At last my breathing slowed, and the trembling subsided. I wiped the sweat from my forehead with the arm of my t-shirt, soaking it. My legs still felt like spaghetti, so I decided the best place for me to finish the night was right where I was. So I closed my eyes and forced myself to drift back to sleep.

The morning dawned like all the rest since the weather had gone crazy—overcast and humid. And the dull sunrise found me where I'd settled, behind the door. Rising, I stretched, trying to take out the kinks the night had left me. I remembered that my first night in Korea had been that way too. I had slept on the floor instead of my bunk, trying to avoid the incoming artillery. It wasn't a matter of courage; it was a matter of being comfortable. Sometimes you had to work yourself into whatever you were about to face.

The four slugs had gone through the bed and into the wall behind. All were large caliber, judging from the holes they left. I pulled the sheet off and looked through the tears. I hoped my brother had some extras, 'cause I needed a change of bedding.

Still barefoot and with the .45 in hand, I did a quick recon of the rest of the house, trying to make sense out of what had happened last night. Somebody had wanted me dead, but why?

Answers didn't seem to be real plentiful, so I padded back to the bedroom and decided to shower and get dressed before somebody else tried to kill me. No uniform today. Khaki pants and shirt, with my automatic in the shoulder holster. A jacket to cover the gun, my old, gray fedora and heavy, ground-pounder boots with my knife tucked into the top. I felt a bit silly, but after last night, I was pretty sure today wasn't going to be any joy ride.

I checked the Packard over from top to bottom, but it didn't seem to have been tampered with. All the rust was still in place. But I do have to admit, it was with some trepidation that I turned the key. When it roared to life and I was still in one piece, I unscrewed my face, opened my eyes, and backed out onto the street. It might have been a coincidence, but seconds after I started down the street, a patrol car passed me going the other way, and I could have swore his eyes were bigger and rounder than they had any right to be.

I grabbed some greasy eggs at a diner, and then with a pencil-drawn map, the Packard and I were humming down the highway, headed out of town.

The ten miles flashed by quickly. And after I followed the road to the lab site, I don't think I was quite prepared for what I saw. I'd seen buildings destroyed by bombs, some of which I'd dropped, but they were nothing like this. There was nothing left! Not a stick or a stone left standing. All that was there was a crater in the ground—a hole, where tiny bits of debris had fallen back down. Only the fence around the outside was intact.

I pulled inside the gate and put the Packard to sleep. Then with a sigh, I pushed open the door and got out. Even with the heavy cloud cover, the day was warming fast; I could feel sweat starting to bead up around my hat band and under my arms. The cinders of the drive crunched under my feet as I walked over to where the building had once stood. No two pieces were still connected.

As I kicked through the detritus that had been the last moments of my brother's life—bits of wood, chunks of brick and twisted steel, none of it any bigger than my fist—something struck me as odd. Everything in the hole was charred and burned like it had been cooked in a giant oven. And it wasn't until I came to what had been the back of the building that something else struck me…there was nothing, no debris at all, outside what had been the actual perimeter of the building. There had been a gigantic explosion that reduced the building to pretty much dust, but nothing had been blown outside. You could still see the line where the structure stopped and the lot began.

This had to have been one fantastic fireball. A fireball so intense that it literally melted everything. Gas explosions were hot, but nothing like this. Even Dresden hadn't burned like this. Only Hiroshima and Nagasaki had been this hot.

I must have been pretty intent on what I was doing, because I didn't hear him approach until he was almost on top of me. I came up off of one knee with the automatic in my hand and pointed at his midsection. And what a midsection it was. He was a pear with feet, like those balloons they give kids at supermarket openings. He must have been around forty-five or fifty, with a bad comb over, hound dog jowls, and rheumy, red eyes that were about twice their normal size at the moment. He had his fat hands in front of him as though warding off a bullet. "Don't shoot me! I'm the one that belongs here," he squeaked. "Who are you and why are you here?"

I let the gun sink until it was pointed at the ground. "I'm Owen's brother. The sheriff said you were both out of town."

"I just got back this morning and came out to see what was left." He looked around and shook his head. "Gas explosions are terrible things."

"Except even a gas explosion doesn't do this." I swept the hole with the gun. "A gas explosion is like a bomb going off inside a building. Everything gets blown outward. This incinerated everything right where it was. Sort of like the sun sat on it."

"But the Sheriff said—"

I cut him off. "I think he was just way too comfortable in his office to even come out here and take a look." I switched gears, trying to trip him up a bit. "Do you know why somebody would want my brother dead, Doctor…?"

The thought of someone having killed Owen turned him a bit green. "Hansen. Doctor Hansen. I don't know of any reason anybody would want your brother dead, Mr. Steele. Nothing we were doing was important enough to warrant anything like this. We don't even have a government contract right now. We've just been doing little stuff for a couple of appliance firms."

"Well he called me a couple of days ago, fairly excited, and said that he was in trouble. Do you know why anybody would be after him? Or maybe what, specifically, he was working on?"

He shook his bulb-shaped head. "No, I don't. You know how closed-mouthed your brother could be about his work."

This man didn't know Owen at all. There was nothing he loved more than talking about his work and himself. I was about to tell him so, but a big, red spot appeared in the middle of his forehead, and he went flying backward.

The second silenced shot tore the epaulet off my jacket. And by the third shot, the spot I was standing in was empty, and I was rolling in the dirt with the .45 cocked and ready. I had a general idea where he might be hiding, but by the time I got my bearings, he could have moved. I dug down into the remains of the building as deep as I could, waited for the next shot, and hoped I still had my head when it was over.

Suddenly two craters of dirt popped up in front of me, and I had him! There was a small pile of rocks and a scrub bush just outside the gate. I'd seen him duck back down after he fired the last time. I sucked in a deep breath, held it, and sighted just over the rock pile. Like a puppet show, he popped up again for just a second, and my automatic barked twice. And as the prize for my careful diligence, I heard his gun clatter down on the rocks.

I gave him a couple more seconds to make sure that he was down. Then I climbed to my feet and, keeping low, made my way over to where he was laying. One of the bullets had caught him in the shoulder. Far from fatal, but it was enough pain to put him down. I kicked his gun off the rocks and away from him. Looked just about like the gun that tried to put holes in this sleeping beauty last night.

I had started to go around the rocks when the back of my skull seemed to explode into light. As I toppled to the ground, I cursed my own stupidity. The gunman wasn't alone.

CHAPTER 3

I awoke to pain and the feeling of motion. The pain was good; it meant that I wasn't dead. But the motion was something else altogether. Why should I be moving if I were lying in the dirt? Slowly I cracked my eyelids, figuring that the light would blind me and split my head open. But that first glance at what was going on popped them open like fresh corn!

I was in the front seat of the Packard, which was going faster than any Packard had the right to go, and was headed straight towards a rapidly approaching horizon. That could only mean one of two things. Either the Packard was about to go into space, or it was about to drop off the edge of the world! And since Packards don't fly...

Even through the pain, my flight training took over. I kicked out the stick that was holding down the foot feed, jerked the wheel hard to the left, and stomped down hard on the brake pedal with both feet.

The big car slewed sideways in a cloud of dust, and for a moment, I lost sight of the horizon. But I never let go of the wheel or let pressure off the brake. Finally the engine chugged and died, and with it the momentum ran out. It rocked forward on its tired springs, and then it fell still.

All the while, I'd been holding my breath, but now it whistled out through my teeth. I clicked off the ignition, pushed open the door, and rolled out onto the running board.

For a long time I just sat there, breathing. Finally, when I stopped trembling, I took stock. The back of my head was a swollen, sore, sticky mess. My gun was gone, but I still had the car. Not so great a trade, but it meant I didn't have to walk. And I had the pain to remind me just how stupid I had been back there, and how lucky I was to be alive.

I pushed myself up off the running board and walked around the car to make sure all the parts were still connected. It was sitting about three feet from a hole that was deeper than the Chrysler building was tall—the edge of the world! I felt my stomach roll at the thought of going over. I swallowed hard twice, wiped my hand across my mouth, and climbed back into the car.

This was twice now, and I intended to see that it didn't happen a third time. Whoever they were, they were going to regret leaving me alive!

* * * * *

When I got to the lab site, my gun and my hat were right where they'd fallen, but neither Hansen nor the man I shot were. That made me shake my head, which made it hurt. Why take Hansen's body with them? I blew the sand out of the automatic's action, picked up my hat, and walked back to the car. As I fired it up and turned back towards town, the radio reminded me how much worse the weather was getting.

* * * * *

As Captain Steele turned back towards town, another car was just pulling up behind a combination office and warehouse on the edge of the business district. What made it unusual was that the driver had a big, red spot in the middle of his forehead like he had been shot. His companion was built like a pro-wrestler, but one of his wings was in a sling. Blood was slowly staining it red. The man with the red spot shut off the car and turned to the other one. "What now?"

"I guess we tell him what happened and hope we walk out alive. After all, we did take care of the problem."

"Maybe we should have stayed to make sure that he was dead."

"He was out of it! There's no way he could have woke up and saved himself."

The man with the spot pushed open the door and got out. The wrestler did the same on his side, wincing in pain. "But what if he did?"

The big man with his arm in a sling shook his head as he walked up to the steel door. "If he did, we'll have to deal with it later. Just don't tell *him* that, or we'll be out there scouring the desert looking for him—if we're still alive." Then, he punched a special series of numbers into the pad beside the door and waited. Seconds later, the door swung open. Behind it there was only darkness.

As the door opened, they both seemed to choke a bit, and their eyes glazed. Stiffly, they marched through the door and into the inky blackness beyond. Behind them, untouched, it closed by itself. They stumbled a short distance to a second door, which opened before they could reach for the handle. This room was in twilight. But as they entered, two spotlights pointed towards the door came on, blinding them.

Behind the lights, a shadowy, hooded figure was seated at a desk. The dark holes in his hood where his eyes should have been turned towards the two men. And as they did, the holes burned red with an inner fire. "Report!" The voice was cold and mechanical, like death. And the two men shivered in fear.

With his voice shaking, the not-so-dead Hansen spoke. "Sir, the Soldier is dead, sir. We put him in his car and drove it off a cliff."

His partner quickly chimed in, confirming what Hansen had said. "There is no way that he could have gotten out alive. And it'll look just like an accident."

The hooded figure nodded. "Good. It was unfortunate that he got that close to us. But if the threat is gone…"

Together they nodded and said, "It is, sir! You can believe us on that!"

For the first time, he seemed to notice the shape the two of them were in—both covered in dirt, and Hansen with the big, red spot on his forehead. Turning those red pits of eyes towards Hansen, he demanded, "What happened to you? What is that in the middle of your forehead?"

"It was all part of our deception, sir. You see, we wanted the captain…"

His interest in Hansen's story waned fast, and he turned to the man in the sling. "And you?"

"He got the drop on me, sir. But it's nothing. Hansen helped me patch it up." He moved a bit forward and tried to cover up the blood that was dripping on the floor. The man in the hood noticed the movement and saw the blood.

"You're bleeding all over my floor!" he roared. "Get out! Go help with the interrogation!"

Together they spun around and fled from the office. If they had stayed to listen, they would have heard the man in the hood say to himself, "It is unfortunate that you got in the way. But I knew sooner or later you would have to be dealt with. Now I can proceed with my plan." Then he laughed—a laugh that sounded like a cold wind on Halloween.

* * * * *

This time on the way into town, I stayed off the main streets and wound my way back to Owen's through the alleys.

I thought it might be a good thing if they went on thinking I was dead for a while. When I got within a block of his house, I parked the car and made it the rest of the way on foot. I went in through the back door and pulled down all the window shades.

After a little work on the back of my head and half a bottle of aspirin, I felt a bit better. It was time to plan my next move. I still had no idea who "they" were, but now I knew for sure that "they" existed. But why had they killed Owen, and why were they trying to kill me? Too many questions and not enough answers. There was only one man who might be able to give me any answers at all, and I had no idea where he was. But as somebody once told a little girl, the best place to begin is at the beginning.

I decided to try Gallagher's apartment. Using my magnificent detective skills, I found the phonebook and looked up the address. I quickly retraced my steps back outside, and minutes later, the Packard and I were headed back across town. Off to the north I could see the dark, rolling clouds of another storm beginning to form. For a second, it made me wonder why the weather here wasn't affected. Then I came up on Gallagher's block and didn't think any more about it. I had other fish to fry.

I turned onto the tree-lined street, rolled the collar of my jacket up, and with a wince of pain, pulled my hat down. Slumping lower in the seat, I cruised past the lone vehicle parked along the curb. The man sitting inside didn't give me a second glance, but I looked him over good.

He was your typical, beefy thug—unshaven, cheap suit, leaning against the door of the car intent on the front door of the apartment building. I eased on past. Half a block later, I pulled into an alley and followed it back to the red brick building. I brought the Packard to a stop behind the building and carefully removed the dome light with the butt of my .45. Then I slid out the door and into the growing twilight.

The service entrance was locked, but after a couple of pushes with my shoulder, it popped open. The groan of the jam tearing loose gave me a few seconds of fright, but it must have gone unheard, because nobody came to investigate. I let my breath out and stepped inside. I seemed to be in some kind of washer room. Clotheslines crisscrossed the room, and a couple of automatic washers stood along the wall. The room smelled of bleach and detergent, and I felt a sneeze building. With my nose squeezed tight between my fingers, I made a beeline across the room and out into the hall. Just as I cleared the stair door, it caught up with me. I suppressed the sneeze, but I thought my head was going to explode!

The information I'd gotten from the phonebook said he lived in apartment 3D. So staying near the outside of the steps, I started up, taking the light bulbs out as I went. I wasn't going to make myself any bigger of a target than I had to. When I reached the third floor, I eased the door open and stuck my head out. The tenant in the first apartment had either the radio or television on and turned up so loud that I could have fired off my automatic without anybody hearing me. To me that meant, unless the rest of the apartments were soundproof, that the floor was empty.

When I got to 3D, I stuck my penlight in my mouth and went to work on the lock. No shoulder this time; I needed a bit of finesse. I might as well have not bothered. I bumped the door with my arm and it swung inward, unlocked. I rose to my feet, and with my gun in hand and my flashlight still in my mouth, I carefully stepped across the threshold into the darkened room. And for the second time I felt the back of my head explode. For an instant I was in pain, and then I slumped to the floor, uncaring.

CHAPTER 4

Slowly, consciousness returned and brought with it, like before, blinding pain. But this time there was no sense of motion. Twice in one day was way too much for my poor head. I figured it must have looked a lot like a smashed pumpkin. I raised my hand to feel it, but I found that I couldn't. Either I'd lost control of my arm, or somebody had me tied to a chair. Tied to a chair?! I forced open my eyes and swore to God that I was looking into the sun! I closed them again, rolled them around behind their lids, and then opened them once more.

This time it was better. I was sitting, tied to a chair, and somebody had a desk light pointed at my face. That "somebody" was sitting there in front of me, behind the light, pointing my .45 at my chest. When I moved, I got poked with the gun, and a woman's voice said, "Move and I'll ventilate you!"

I'm sure my face screwed up into disbelief. "Ventilate? What is this, a serial?"

She poked me again with the gun. "I mean I'll shoot you!"

I think being hit twice in one day was making me a bit giddy, because I looked down, chuckled a bit, and said, "Well, if you're going to shoot me, you should probably take the safety off. And could you move the light? I'd hate to die blind."

I knew she was fuming, because I heard her growl. I heard the safety click just before she poked me again, but the light moved and my eyeballs started to cool down. "Are you going to poke me to death? Or shoot me?"

31

Fuming was right; she practically spit her next question. "Who are you and what are you doing here?"

No reason for me to lie to her, so I said, "I'm Captain Rick Steele, and I'm looking for Professor Gallagher."

She made to poke me again, and then she seemed to think the better of it. "Why? And your answer had better be good, or I'm gonna give you another hole to breathe through."

It was all I could do now to stop from laughing at her tough-guy act. "There's a knife in my boot that'll poke holes in me a lot faster than that gun. Might even say it was made for that." She made to hit me with the gun, and I quickly said, "The Professor worked with my brother out on the mesa, and I'm trying to find out what happened. I thought maybe he might have some information. If you're him, you're not at all what I expected."

She pulled the gun back and used the front sight to push back a lock of hair that had fallen across her forehead, like she was thinking over what I said. Finally she decided. "No, I'm not. I'm his daughter. When I heard what had happened and I couldn't reach him, I came looking for him. I found him gone and the apartment like this." She swept the room with the gun. Chairs were overturned; the coffee table was smashed. Just a general mess everywhere. Either the Professor had a really lousy housekeeper, or there'd been a fight. Looked a bit like he'd done himself proud.

"Now that we've been introduced, do you think you could untie me?"

She thought that over for a minute too. This girl was a deep thinker. But then she took a knife—my knife, the one from my boot—and cut me loose. "But I'm keeping the gun, and you'd better not try to run away!"

"I'm not even sure I can stand up, much less try to run away!" I wobbled to my feet and felt the back of my head. Not much worse than before. But at this rate, if I was going to live, I was going to have to start wearing a steel helmet. "I don't suppose you have any aspirin?"

She was going to argue with me, but then she remembered that my pain was her fault, so she went off in search of a pain reliever. While she was gone, I took a look around the room. I was right; it had been quite a struggle. But that wasn't what interested me. What caught my attention was in an alcove the Professor had been using for his home office, just off the kitchen. It was a desk that was piled with books, sketches of scientific devices, scrawled notes, and newspaper clippings. Some were yellowed with age, but some were as fresh as last week. They all concerned just two things: the weather changes and flying saucers. I felt like I was back in my brother's room again. Whatever was going on, they both had been following the same line.

I pulled out the chair, slumped down into it, and started to read. The town seemed to have been a hotbed of saucer activity since back in the thirties—lights in the sky, disappearances, strange occurrences. But after the war, it all seemed to have stopped. Then in the last couple of months, the strange lights were back. According to his notes, each sighting meant a weather crash up north. And they were growing in frequency. I squeezed my head in my hands to hold in the pain and shook it. Barely aloud I asked, "What did you boys get yourselves into?"

"Apparently more than they could handle from the looks of things." She had come up behind me while I was reading, and I hadn't heard her. She was holding out a glass of water and my aspirin.

Eagerly I swallowed the tablets and drained the glass to wash them down. Then, for the first time, I took a really good look at her, and I almost whistled.

She was almost as tall as me with auburn hair that fell softly over her shoulders; its fingers reached down and caressed the gentle upturn of her breasts. Oval face, high cheek bones, and lush, full lips that had a natural pout—a bit like a kiss just waiting for some place to go. Long lashes shielded the fire in her blue eyes that tried to drag you in. She was dressed in a khaki blouse, blue jeans rolled at the cuffs, and heavy boots. This girl was no cream puff.

"So, what now? Do you have any idea where my dad might be?"

"Well, Miss Gallagher—" I didn't get a chance to finish my thought before she interrupted me.

"Actually, it's Doctor Gallagher. Doctor Katherine M. Gallagher. 'Kate' to my friends, but I doubt you'll ever have to worry about that." I felt a smile spread across my face. "A Ph.D. in anthropology. Currently the head of New Mexico State's Anthropology Department. I was on a dig a couple hundred miles from here when I heard what happened. So I rushed over."

"Well, Doctor Gallagher," I started again. "There's a man out front in a blue Ford watching this building. I don't know if he's looking for you or for me, but he's looking. And I'm willing to bet he knows where your father is." *If he's still alive*, I thought to myself. Instead I said, "And I intend to go out there and ask him that very question."

"Then you'll probably need this." She handed the Colt back, and I flicked the safety back on and slid it into my shoulder holster.

"Here's my idea, and hopefully it won't get either one of us killed." She leaned in close and I told her my plan.

* * * * *

34

The thug in the car was listening to the radio, so he had no idea what was going on behind him until the eminent Dr. Gallagher walked up on the passenger side, stuck her head in the window, and asked, "Hey bud, got a light?"

He was busy fumbling for a match to accommodate her when I walked up and stuck the .45 in his ear. His body got real stiff all of a sudden, and his hand kind of hovered near his belt while he tried to make up his tiny mind. I wasn't willing to wait, so I made the decision for him. "If you'd like a nice, new tunnel all the way through your head, go ahead and reach for it. I'm pretty sure I can pull my trigger faster than you can pull your gun," I whispered in my scariest voice.

He must have believed me, because he went limp and slumped back deeper into the seat. "Now, very carefully put both your tiny, little paws on the wheel where we can see them, and the nice lady will take your gun. If you so much as breathe, she'll have to go home and take a shower to get your brains off of her, and it'll probably cost me a new blouse. Right, Doll?"

Her eyes narrowed a bit at the use of the nickname, but she pulled open the door and reached to retrieve his gun. He waited until she was half in the car and leaning across before he made his move. With one hand, he reached out and grabbed the front of her blouse, dragging her towards him while shoving his feet against the floor and knocking the automatic away with his shoulder.

I struggled to get a grip on him through the window but couldn't find anything to get a real hold on as he squirmed in the seat. I thought he must be seeing open sky and wasn't slowing down.

What he didn't figure on was that the sweet-looking girl was more than he bargained for. Even as he was jerking her towards him, she was pushing herself forward and on top of him. As she did, she brought the heal of her hand up under his chin hard enough that I could hear his teeth clack. As his head went back, she drove her knee into his groin and her other hand into his midsection. Just as suddenly as it started, it was over, and he fell back against the door. "Don't kill him, damn it! He's still got to talk!"

Kate wasn't much for listening. She stuck two fingers in his nostrils and pulled hard enough to bring tears of pain to his bloodshot eyes. "I want to know where my dad is! Lie to me and your nose'll look like a bat."

While she was threatening him, I pulled a twin to my .45 out of his belt. I could feel him trembling. "Who's your old man," he stuttered.

She pushed a little harder, and even I winced. "Professor Gallagher." There was a wet spot growing on the front of his pants.

"They're holding him at the Stevens Building downtown. He's being moved out at midnight. Please, Mister. Don't let her kill me!" It was a good thing that I was behind him so he couldn't see my grin. But then after that performance in the front seat, I wasn't too sure about her myself.

So instead of saying anything, I brought the automatic down against the back of his head and put him to sleep. As he slumped forward against the wheel, Kate slid out the other side. Over the roof I said, "That was quite a tough-girl act you put on. Not to mention the punches. Where'd you learn to fight like that?"

"Spent most of my life in a man's world. So I had to know how to defend myself. Had an old family friend that was a paratrooper, and he taught me a few things. And besides, who said I was acting?"

I faked a shudder, and as we walked around the back of the car, I handed her the thug's gun. "Well, if you fight like a man, I hope you can shoot like one too."

Those pretty lips broke into a smile, and fire flashed in her eyes. "Call me 'Doll' again, and you'll be the first to find out!"

"Yes Ma'am."

* * * * *

The room was nearly dark, and the hooded figure was seated behind his desk once more. His dark suit made him almost invisible as Hansen and his partner brought the old man into the room. Each one of them had an arm, and they dragged him across the floor, the toes of his shoes leaving a trail. The man was in his early sixties with a shock of unruly, gray hair, made even messier by the blood that was matting it down in places. There was also blood under his nose and down the front of his shirt. He was barely conscious.

As they approached the desk, the man in the hood rose to meet them. He walked around to the front of the desk, and taking the old man's chin in his hand, he raised his head. "You are being quite difficult, Professor. Who would have thought an old man like you could have such stamina." His voice was like that of a snake, if a snake could talk.

Slowly the Professor opened his one unswollen eye and looked up into the masked face. And then with all the strength he had left, he spit at it!

The masked man roared, and with spittle dripping off his hood, he lashed out at the Professor with a backhand that sent him flying across the room. He walked across the room and kicked him hard in the ribs. Then he regained his composure. "No matter, Professor. Where we're taking you, we have better methods of gaining your cooperation." Then turning to the other two, he said, "Take him downstairs and prepare him for the trip. We will be leaving for the ranch in about half an hour." Finished with them, he turned, walked back behind the desk, did something with the wall, and was gone.

They walked over, picked up the old man once again, and dragged him out of the room.

* * * * *

The Packard slid through the darkened streets of town like a green phantom. If not for the squeaks and rattles it had picked up in the desert, I'd have felt like the Green Hornet powering the Black Beauty across town.

When I got about three blocks from the building we were looking for, I pulled the car to the curb and shut it off. Reaching across her, I pushed Kate's door open. "This is as far as you go. It's gonna get real hot around here real soon, and I want you out of the way."

She sat up straight in the seat and fought to pull the door shut. "No, you're not leaving me behind. I can handle myself as well as any man. Besides, it's my father."

"And I'm quite sure that he would like very much to see you again—alive!"

She started to protest again, and I rubbed my aching head in my hands. Then I threw my hands in the air in resignation. "Fine, then. I don't have time to argue. Just stay out of the way!" I threw the Packard into gear and roared off, spitting gravel. Seconds later we were pulling into the alley behind the building.

I cocked the .45 and pushed open my door. She did the same on the other side of the car. "Keep behind me," I hissed, and she nodded. Then we moved off into the alley, trying to stay covered as best we could.

From garbage can to dumpster, dumpster to trash pile, we tried to stay out of sight until we reached the alley door.

There was a large flatbed truck, a tarp covering whatever it was carrying, idling in the alley. As I watched, two men in coveralls came out, climbed into the cab, and drove off into the darkness. Seconds later, a newer model Lincoln slid to a stop in the just-vacated spot. Two men got out; one of them was literally a pear with feet. He had what looked like the remains of a big, red spot on his forehead that he kept trying to wipe away. Hansen! He had suckered me big time, and I'm betting I owed him for the first dent in my skull.

The other man was taller, better built, and had one arm in a sling—the man I'd shot! They left the car running and went into the building. Moments later they emerged, half carrying and half dragging a white-haired old man between them. I turned to ask Kate if that was her father, but she was gone! Suddenly a shot rang out, and a new spot appeared in Hansen's forehead. This time he wasn't going to get back up.

The man with the sling dropped the old guy and scrabbled for his own gun as Kate's second shot went wide, chewing up the brick behind him. About that time the door flew open again, and two more men with guns emerged. I had no choice but to open fire.

My first shot sent one of the new gunmen hurtling back through the door, while Kate put another one down. While she was keeping them pinned down, I came up with a quickie plan. I got behind the dumpster, and using it like shield, I started pushing it across the alley towards the door. Kate must have figured out what I was up to, because she slid back across the alley to give me a hand. The dumpster hurtled across the pavement like a tank, just missing the prone figure of her father on the ground and smashing into the thugs. As it banged into them and then hit the side of the building, we went tumbling onto our butts too. We both quickly rolled to our bellies with guns extended, but they had the dumpster on top of them and weren't moving to get up. We grabbed the unconscious old man and dragged him back across the alley.

Just as we were ducking for cover again, a man wearing a black hood ran out of the door and leaped into the waiting car. The remaining thug, firing as he ran, followed suit and slid behind the wheel. In a squeal of tires and a cloud of blue exhaust, they raced out of the alley.

Again I turned to say something to Kate, but she was gone. And just as I was about to start cussing, the Packard streaked into the alley and slammed to a stop. The passenger door flew open, and she hollered, "Get him in the car! We can still catch them!"

I lifted up the frail old man and sort of tossed him in the seat between us. Then I started to climb in, but she wasn't waiting. I still had one foot on the street when we roared off after the Lincoln. We came out of the alley and onto the street on two wheels. Somewhere in the distance I heard the low whine of police sirens. "Is he alright?" she yelled over the engine.

I felt for a pulse and looked him over. He was in his middle sixties with a harder version of Kate's face. Somebody had worked him over pretty good, but he was alive. "He's hurting, but I think he'll make it!" Her only answer was a nod and a harder push on the accelerator. In the distance I could just see the taillights of the other car.

Little by little, as the streets flew by under us, we started to gain on the other car. Since we were traveling without lights, I don't even think they knew we were behind them until I leaned out the window and fired a shot. The back window of the Lincoln spider-webbed as the bullet tore through it.

It must have startled the driver pretty good! The big car suddenly swerved left, then back right, coming up on two wheels as he fought to bring it back under control. It leaped across the sidewalk, sideswiped a tree, and then darted back out onto the street as he mastered it once more.

As they slewed back into the street, Kate took advantage of their misstep and pulled nearly abreast. I was about to put another bullet into the car when the hooded figure in the back leaned out and opened fire, making both of us duck. The bullet plowed through our windshield and struck the seat next to the Professor. Dropping back, she slammed into the car. The screech of metal tearing was nearly deafening. I had to catch myself on the dash to stop from ending up on the floor.

I leaned out the window as she slammed our bumper into theirs and pumped three slugs into their trunk compartment, hoping to hit the gas tank. But no such luck. We had long since passed out of town and were racing across the desert. Clouds of sand and dust were rolling out from under the two cars as we tore through the night. Then suddenly, the odds all changed. An ear-splitting whine filled the car. And as an eerie, green light enveloped us, the Packard coughed and began to slow. Kate stomped on the starter, but there was no response. It had become nothing more than a rock rolling slowly across the desert.

I leaned out the window and a scream of disbelief was torn from my throat. "Son of a…" My mind could hardly comprehend what I was looking at. Above us, so close that I could feel the heat and smell the ozone, was something from another world—a great oval-shaped ship, glowing bright green and spinning like a kid's top! Above the bottom saucer shape I could make out the bubble of what I assumed was the bridge.

I slid back into the seat, my face a mass of confusion, my eyes big and round. I looked over to Kate and shook my head.

"This thing just got bigger than we could have ever imagined. There's a flying saucer over our heads." Almost as soon as the words were out of my mouth, it shot ahead of us to the Lincoln. A door in the bottom opened, and what looked like an electromagnet dropped down and attached itself to the roof of the car. Then seconds later, like a fisherman with his catch, the car was reeled into the bottom of the ship. The opening closed, and it streaked off over the horizon. We couldn't do anything but sit there and watch them disappear. Shortly after they were gone, the lights on the Packard came back on.

I jumped out and emptied my gun out of frustration in the direction the saucer had taken. "Damnit! How are we supposed to fight something like that? We're just men!"

Kate calmly got out of the car, walked over, and took my gun out of my hand. "We fight it the same way we always have—with guts and determination. Just because they have better aircraft than we do, it doesn't mean they're smarter."

I stared at her in disbelief, and finally she shrugged. "Okay then, maybe smarter. But not braver!" Then she started back towards the car. "So what's the plan now?"

"Well, there's a little town a few miles from here that I'm hoping is out of their sphere of influence. We'll get a room there and hole up for a while, and figure out what to do next. I think we're gonna need some help. And I think your dad could use some attention." In the car, the old man moaned, almost like he agreed with me.

* * * * *

The cargo bay closed beneath the Lincoln, and it settled hard onto the deck. Strange-looking beings scurried around it like ants, securing it to the steel plating. They had unusually long arms and thin, almost bird-like legs. Their faces were long, almost triangular-shaped, with high foreheads and pointy chins, and shocks of unruly, red hair covered the tops of their heads. The cargo bay rang with the sound of their strange language.

The man in the hood ignored them as he leaped from the car, dragging the driver out with him. He grabbed him around the throat with one hand, throttling him. "You swore that he was dead! That dead man almost killed me!"

The thug's only reply was a gurgle deep in his throat as he tried to draw a breath. The Hood shook him again and then tossed him to the deck in disgust. Then before he stormed out, he growled, "Make for the ranch. I need to talk to the people upstairs."

CHAPTER 5

The voice of the weather announcer had a harried quality and a bit of hopelessness to it. He rubbed his hand across his chin and leaned in closer to the microphone. "The weather continues to defy all explanation. In the upper Midwest, torrential rains and hail storms have reduced the crops to mere fields of stubble, leaving lakes where days ago corn grew. Most of Manhattan is still at a standstill from the twin tornados that tore through midtown yesterday, virtually shutting down the world financial market.

"In Washington, Senator Joe McCarthy has stated that he suspects that this is some form of first strike by the Communists in preparation for an invasion. Thus far, the President has refused to comment on the senator's statement. Stay tuned for further information as it happens."

The on-air light blinked out, and the weatherman slumped forward with his head on his arms. How much more of this could he take? Then he pulled himself together again and got up to get his forecast ready. He had to be back on the air again in twenty minutes.

* * * * *

The town was so small that it really didn't deserve a spot on the map, but it would serve our purposes well enough. There was a diner, a post office and store, a few houses, and a rundown motor court. It was into the motor court that I piloted the Packard.

The sign out front read "Vacancy," and somehow I doubted that the "No" had ever been lit. An old man with his nightshirt tucked into his pants showed up to open the door when I rang the bell. I'm pretty sure his sleep being disturbed didn't happen every day. He was set to complain, but when he got a good look at the color of my money, he was all smiles.

I came back with the key and told Kate to follow me with the car. I could hear the crunch of the gravel under the tires as we crept across the lot. It had cost me twice the normal room rate, but I had gotten the one farthest from the office to assure us what little privacy the place had to offer.

It was pretty seedy. The carpet was worn through in a few places, and what looked like centuries of smokers had turned the paint from white to a yellowish brown. While Kate stood in the door turning up her nose, I checked out the room and then pushed open the connecting door with my shoulder. It was a carbon copy of this room, only reversed. "We come and go through this room and stay next door. It won't give us much of a margin, but every second counts."

I got her father out of the car and carried him inside, laying him gently on the bed. Whatever drugs they had used on him were starting to wear off a bit, but he was still pretty far gone.

Kate came in and sat down on the bed next to him. Her long fingers pushed the fallen hair from his forehead and stroked his cheek. When she looked up, there was a tear in the corner of her blue eyes. "He's way too old for any of this. I tried to talk him into retiring and coming with me, but he refused. Said 'I'm a scientist, not an excavator!' When I found out what he was doing down here, I figured it would be okay. Small operation, nothing big or secret, so he could take it easy.

"Now look what's happened. Kidnapped by a gang of thugs, drugged, almost shot! Yeah, his life's way easier." She shook her head in despair.

I reached out and squeezed her shoulder. "Its okay, Kate. He's with us now, and I'm not going to let anything happen to him." I tossed a couple of spare clips for the automatic on the bed. "You keep an eye on him, and I'll go down to the diner and get us all something to eat."

She flashed me just the smallest hint of a smile as I walked out the door and said, "Thanks, Rick. For everything."

As I trotted across the highway to the diner, it was my turn to shake my head. What a girl! Looks, brains, brave as hell, and she could drive like a man. Just the girl I'd been looking for all my life. And when she finally showed up, neither one of us was sure we would live to see another day.

The diner was one of those places that looked like a subway car. How it got clear out here in the middle of the desert, I had no idea. Must have been the express. Behind the counter a blonde in a pink uniform, with a couple strands of hair in search of a wash job sneaking out from under her cap, was trying to look busy polishing coffee cups. I doubted her customers ever noticed that they could see themselves in them.

I swung onto the stool, and she made me wait until she was done with the one she was working on. Then she ambled over, and around a wad of gum, asked me what I wanted. Just think—some sweet boy would probably show up in an hour or so to take her home, hoping to play house in the front seat of the car. Poor guy!

I ordered sandwiches and fries to go and a six pack of bottles. While I waited, she poured coffee for me in one of her freshly polished cups. There was food stuck to the side of it.

While I waited for the food, I got some change and walked over to the payphone in the corner. Quickly I dialed the base and asked to talk to Joey, my crew chief. He'd know better than anybody what the situation was. "Joey, this Rick. I need some help, big time. Who's the OOD?"

"I don't know what you've done, but you're in big trouble, Captain. The general's all up in arms. Something about arresting you on sight! And that you were armed and could be dangerous."

I let my breath whistle out between my teeth. "Damn! I can't explain right now, Joey. But whatever they're saying I did, I didn't. Soon as I can tell you more, I will." There was some more small talk, but then I hung up. It just kept getting better and better.

The fries were already soaking the bag with grease by the time I paid my bill and picked it up. The smell was heaven, but after talking to Joey, my appetite was pretty much gone.

As I walked out the door, the girl clicked out the "Never" part of the sign, and now it read just plain "Closed." I guess it was wrong. She picked up the phone as I walked across the road again. Probably calling that boy for a ride.

Kate was toweling her hair dry, and her father was showing a few more signs of life. There was a freshly scrubbed beauty to her face that almost took my breath away. I covered as best I could with the food. "Don't know how good it is, but it's hot!"

She came across the room, wrapping the towel around her head like a turban. "Great. With a shower and some food, I'm starting to feel almost human again." Her blue eyes roamed over me from head to foot, and her nose curled just a bit. "You could use a little humanity yourself you know."

She was right. I wasn't much to look at right now. Blood ran down the back of my neck from being hit on the head twice, and sand was all the way to my shorts from rolling around in the desert. Yep, I could use a little of that humanity. I grabbed one of the beers and headed for the bathroom.

Not sure which was better—the cold beer or the steamy warmth of the shower. I let the water pound against me as it flushed the aches and pains down the drain. I just wished I could have solved our problems as easily.

I was just pulling my boots back on when I heard her outside the door. "Rick? I think you'd better come out here. I think we might have trouble."

I grabbed my automatic and the holster from the towel bar. I hurried into the inner room and up to the window. Sure enough, we had company. There were three cars in the lot and men were spreading out to surround the room that we weren't in.

She came up next to me to look out, and our shoulders touched. They must have been able to see the burst of electricity all the way to Mexico. The scent of her was almost intoxicating. I took a deep breath to clear my head, but it only made it worse. Finally she brought me back to reality. "So what do we do?" she whispered.

I glanced across the room before I spoke. Her father was sitting up on the edge of the bed, chewing on a burger. "Can he travel under his own power?"

"Some."

I chewed on my lip while I thought about it. Then I knew there wasn't much choice. "Take him and go out through the bathroom window." I'd parked the Packard out back earlier, just in case. "I'm going to fire some shots at them and do my best to hold them off. I want you to put him in the car and get the hell out of here. As soon as it's clear, I'll follow you. We can meet up later at my brother's."

She started to argue, but the look on my face stopped her. "We don't have any choice, Kate. You've got to get your father out of here. He's the only one who knows what's really going on. Like I said, I'll come as soon as I can."

There wasn't time for any more argument; they were almost up to the door. She turned to go and then stopped, turned back, and so quickly that I could have missed it, pressed her lips to mine. "For luck!" And she was gone, half carrying her father towards the bathroom.

I moved into the other room, and without even aiming, I opened fire. The men in the parking lot dove into the dirt and ducked behind their cars. I fired a couple more rounds and was about to make my way for the bathroom window when the Packard came flying around the corner of the motel, slewing gravel and blowing blue smoke. And then it streaked off down the highway. I cursed her under my breath for trying to draw them off so I could get away.

Whatever her plan was, it had the desired effect. Orders were shouted, and the men started for the cars. But I couldn't let that happen. So I opened fire, picking off anybody who moved. It worked for a few minutes, but then somebody got smart and slid into one of the cars from the passenger side. Hiding below the window level, he pulled away from the rest and turned to follow her. I put a couple of slugs in the trunk, but it didn't slow him down.

When he took off down the road, the rest of the crew decided it was time to rush me and opened fire on the room. I snapped off a couple of cover shots without looking, and then I rolled into the adjoining room. I pressed my back up against the wall and waited.

I heard the door crash open, then nothing for a few seconds. Then one of them opened fire on the room with what sounded like a submachine gun. Then silence again as they waited. When nothing happened, the three of them entered the room. I heard one of them cross the room and pull the same tactic with the bathroom. Then they noticed the door to the room I was in.

I knew what to expect now—kick open the door, spray the room with bullets, and then enter. I was ready. The instant the door flew open, I rolled out across the floor and opened fire on the machine gunner. As he started to slump forward, I leaped to my feet, crashed into him, and pushed his dead body back into his companions.

The first one went down with the dead man on top of him, but the second was far enough back to leap clear. I didn't wait for the surprise to pass; I fired from the hip and watched a nice, big, red spot appear in the middle of his chest. Like a bag of sand, he folded up onto the floor.

There wasn't time to catch my breath. The other one had freed himself from the dead man and was fumbling for his dropped gun. I drew a bead on him and quickly pulled the trigger. The empty click was like a sonic boom. I dropped my gun and hurled myself at him.

I struck him about mid-waist, and the two of us tumbled back through the doorway into the other room. My shoulder smacked against the door frame as we went through, and I felt my left arm go numb. Quickly, I bored down on him with my weight and tried to pile drive my fist into his face. I heard something crunch and hoped it wasn't my hand. But when he faltered, I knew it had been his nose instead of my knuckles. I brought my knee down on his crotch as hard as I could, all the while pummeling his broken face with my right fist. It seemed like forever, but at last he went limp beneath me, his breath coming in ragged gasps though his crushed nose and bloody lips. My own breath was a burning flame in my throat as I slumped forward on top of him.

For a second or two I lay there and tried to regain what little strength I had left. The feeling was coming back into my arm and shoulder, and I could feel the bruises forming on my ribs where he had been pounding. I straightened my arms to push myself off him, and the left one nearly folded under me. The shoulder was all needles and pins.

Suddenly something jerked at the back of my shirt, and I was literally flying through the room. My back and head hit flat against the wall, dislodging a shower of plaster and dust. Dazed, I slid to the floor, sparks blurring my vision. Through the haze, I saw that the big guy I had shot earlier wasn't as dead as I thought. He was hurt, and he was mad; and all that pain was directed right at me.

He lumbered towards me like a giant bear. His face was twisted in an open-mouthed grimace, spittle and blood dripping from the corners. A roar of rage tore from deep inside him. His arms were outstretched, his claw-like hands searching for my throat.

I was dead; there was no way around it. I didn't have enough strength left to fight off a little guy, let alone a giant. I did the only thing I could. I pushed my body into a sitting position, and with the knife from my boot in hand, I waited to strike my last blow.

Suddenly the door beside me crashed open. There was a loud report, and the big guy suddenly grew a third eye right between his eyebrows. He toppled like a tree, and his head landed between my outstretched legs.

I looked up to see Kate, the smoking gun still in her hand, standing in the doorway. Forcing a smile to my cracked lips, I asked, "Do ya think you coulda waited a couple more minutes? I'm pretty sure I had him on the ropes!"

She walked over and pulled me to my feet, and I tried not to wince at the pain. "A couple more minutes and he'd of eaten you for lunch. Next time you shoot somebody, you'd best make sure they're dead." That instant the Professor chose to make his appearance. He rushed in with one of the Tommy guns in hand and swept it around the room like a search light. Luckily he didn't have his finger on the trigger. I limped over and gently pried it from his hands. "Probably better let me have that, Pops. I've got enough holes in me already today. No sense in temping friendly fire for more."

The room was in shambles—the air cloudy with blue smoke from the guns, furniture smashed, bodies laying everywhere. I walked back into the other room and scooped up my empty gun from the floor. It was then that I noticed that I'd pretty much shot up the cast of a Roy Rogers Western. They were all dressed like movie cowboys—boots, shirts with fringe, and fancy-cut jeans rolled up at the cuffs.

I hollered into the other room. "Kate, Professor, check their wallets. These guys are all cowboys." As I walked back through the door, they were doing the same thing that I was, leafing through the thugs' wallets. "Mine says William Henderson, RS Ranch."

The Professor nodded. "Different name, same location."

"Mine too," Kate chimed in. "Wait a minute." She stopped and took a closer look at her cowboy. She took his chin in her hand and turned his face left, then right, studying his profile. She checked his eyes, lifting the lids, and the shape of his ears— even the texture of his hair. Then she walked over and did the same to the other two.

Standing and brushing the dust from her knees, she shook her head and shuddered. In a flat monotone she said, "They're not human, Rick. They're close, and they could probably pass from a distance or maybe in a fight," the last being directed at me, "but they're not human. Bone structure, eye and ear shape—all wrong. Hair texture is more like vines than hair, and the joints are all wonky."

"So these are the guys from the flying saucer then?"

"That's what I'm guessing."

"Great." I nudged one of them with my boot. "Just when it looks like we've finally gotten a break, everything spins around again."

Kate walked over and looked out the window; it was still clear for now. She said, "We can't stay here much longer. Where to now?"

"I've got an idea. But right now I'm kind of wondering why we haven't heard anything from the clerk. He has to have heard all the noise and seen what happened. Professor, why don't you take a walk over there and see what's going on."

He nodded, and after a longing look at the machine gun I'd taken from him, he went out the door.

"We need to change cars, Kate. We'll take the station wagon these guys came in and ditch the Packard somewhere in the desert."

"That's fine, but you still haven't answered my question. Where are we going?"

"We're heading back to town. Whatever's going on is centered there, and that's where we need to be if we're going to stop it."

"That's fine, but where?"

I was about to tell her when her father came back. He was looking a bit pale and shaken. The bravado he'd displayed before was gone. He came up behind the car and vomited. "Dad, what's happened? Are you alright?"

He stammered a bit before he got out what he wanted to say. "The clerk and some girl are inside the office, dead. Somebody took a knife to them."

"The girl—was she a blonde in a pink waitress dress?"

He retched again but held it in. "I think so. It was hard to tell with so much blood."

53

"If I had to guess, I'd say it was the girl from the diner. I thought she was probably calling her boyfriend when I left, but it looks like she was tipping them off to where we were. And they don't seem to like leaving witnesses." I rubbed my forehead. These guys were playing for keeps, so we had no choice but to play the game the same way. "Kate, you and your dad take the wagon and follow me. When we get a couple of miles out of town, we'll dump this green monster here." I thumped the fender on the Packard with my fist.

I slid into the seat, and releasing a cloud of blue smoke, fired it up. With them following close behind, I powered it down the highway to its last roundup.

CHAPTER 6

The producer gently shook the weatherman awake. He had fallen asleep with his head down on the desk. "It's time again, Bob." He laid the sheets from the teletype down on the desk beside him. Wiping the sleep from his eyes, Bob picked up the latest weather news and headed for the booth. No sooner did he sit down than the on-air light came on. He began to read. "Ladies and gentlemen, this is station PROX coming to you from the flooded streets of downtown and bringing you your weather news.

"The overnight brought relative calm across the upper Midwest, although the flooding continues. Even now, a new front is beginning to build off to the west.

"Seventeen people were killed last night when an earthen levee gave way, sending a wall of water crashing into a church that was being used as a refugee center."

The producer shut off the volume in the room. It was just more of the same bad news. He walked wearily over to the window and looked down on the city. Nothing but the water, lapping halfway up on the first floor windows, moved. The city was dark except for an occasional street light on higher ground that still had power. Off to the east, he could see the capitol with the sun coming up behind it. Were the legislators still there, meeting, trying to find a way to save the people? Or had they all gone home to their own families to wait for the death that was rising to strike them? As he looked out, he became even more certain that he and Bob were the only two people left in the world. Almost in defiance of that thought, the teletype sprang to life, bringing in fresh news. He pulled the sheet from the machine, and what he read made his bloodshot eyes become saucer shaped. Quickly he carried it into the booth and handed it to Bob.

Reading it, Bob gave him a questioning look, but all he could do was shrug. In disbelief he began to read. "Ladies and gentlemen, the President has just declared martial law over the effected territories. He has called out federal troops and instituted a shoot-on-sight policy for looters. All people in the affected areas are being asked to make sure that they are carrying identification at all times. Anyone found without papers will be arrested. This is not a hoax.

"I repeat, the President of the…"

* * * * *

The man in the black hood reached out and shut off his radio. Beneath his mask he was smiling. What they had worked so hard for was finally coming to fruition.

Turning his eyes to the east, he nodded with satisfaction. Seldom had he seen such a magnificent sunrise.

* * * * *

A couple miles from the motor court, I turned the Packard into the desert and cut out across the sand. I topped a small rise, and down on the other side was a stand of scrub trees. I pulled in under them and climbed out. I stood beside it and stroked the roof for a second. It had saved my life more than once, and I was going to miss the beast. We'd almost become a team.

Kate skidded to a stop next to me. "Want me to leave you two alone for a few minutes?"

I got my stuff from the trunk, tossed it into the back seat of the wagon, and slid in beside it. "At least she appreciated me. You just worry about getting us where we're going."

"How can I do that if you haven't told me?"

"Just head back to town and I'll tell you when we get close."

She gave me big harrumph and slammed the wagon into gear. I gripped the back of the seat as she tore out across the sands and headed back to the highway.

We'd gone a couple of miles when I said, "When we get back to town, stay off the main streets and take us back to the building where we found your father."

She slammed on the breaks, throwing her father and me out of the seat. "What?"

Righting myself, I said, "It's the safest place in town. They're not using it, and nobody would ever suspect that we would. It's on the edge of town with lots of room and a garage. It's perfect for us."

As we started off again, I leaned up over the seat. "Professor, are you ready to tell us what you remember?"

He scratched the thinning hair on the back of his head and shrugged his boney shoulders. "I don't remember much of the last two days. I was either being drugged or beaten. I spent most of the time drifting in and out of consciousness."

"What about before they kidnapped you, at the lab? Do you remember any of that?"

He straightened up in the seat. "Of course I do, young man. I may be old, but I'm not senile!" he said, huffily.

I covered my smile with my hand. Like father, like daughter. "I didn't mean that you were, sir. I was just asking."

"Humph." And he turned back to watching the scenery go by. I sat back and waited, but I got only silence.

Finally I prompted him again. "Do you think that you could tell me about it, Professor?"

"Tell you about what?" I was about to explain again, but I saw the smile at the corner of his mouth. Then without looking back, he started to talk, a far-off quality in his tired voice. "It was before the war that I opened the lab. Nothing very big. A few government contracts, but mostly research for appliance companies, UL and the like. Not enough to get rich, but enough to put Kate through college.

"And after her mother died, it was not much more than a hobby. Then your brother Owen showed up looking for a job. I told him that I didn't have anything for him, that we were just a small facility and he was way overqualified for us, but he wouldn't give up. You know how pushy he could be. Said he had contacts and could get us work, and that he had a few ideas of his own that just needed someplace to grow. I tried to tell him no. But then over coffee, it suddenly all became clearer. I guess I got caught up in his enthusiasm.

"Our deal was that he would pay for whatever extra projects he took on, and the lab would share twenty percent of the final profit. Seemed like a good idea to me, and it gave me somebody besides the lab assistants to talk to."

"What about Hansen? Did you have the same deal with him?" I interrupted.

"Hansen?" His face added a couple more wrinkles as he scrunched it up and curled his lip. "Hansen wasn't any more than a floor sweeper. It was his job to clean up whatever messes we made and to hold the bolt from turning."

Then he went back to his story…

* * * * *

The black box stood in the center of the lab. It looked like a concrete bunker with wires coming out of the top. It had a glass door on the front and was surrounded by sandbags.

Long tables and work benches lined the perimeter of the lab, stacked with bits and pieces of electronic equipment in various stages of disarray. Two men in long lab coats were standing next to the box arguing.

One of them was short with thinning, gray hair and in his early sixties. The other was younger, fortyish, with a full head of black hair that came down to a point in the middle of his forehead. His eyes were dark like his hair. And at the moment, the two men were spitting fire at the other.

"I'm telling you Henry, it's too much magnetron," the dark-haired one growled.

"It's not the magnetron. It's the shielding. It's leaking faster than the Titanic! If we patch the shielding…"

"And how do you propose to do that, Henry?"

The old man grinned, showing all his teeth. "We build a detector! Then we fire up the oven, see where it leaks, and patch the holes. And with a detector, we'll be able to measure the amount of radiation we're losing and build the shielding accordingly."

"How long? We're behind on the project already, and I've got things I need to get done."

Henry grinned again. "Two days. Give me two days, and I'll have it." As he walked across the room towards one of the benches, he turned back to Owen. "You know, when you first proposed this partnership, I was against it. But I have to admit that working and thinking has made me feel alive again."

Whatever Owen's answer was, it was mumbled under his breath as he walked the other way across the lab.

True to his word, on the morning of the third day when Owen came to work, Henry was standing in the midst of the

ɔunded by cables. In front of him was what looked
t from a cheap movie, with electrodes sticking out of
the top and mounted on a two-wheeled dolly. He was wearing
his schoolboy grin again. "See Owen, I told you two days. It's
not pretty, but it works."

It was Owen's turn to grin, and he ran his thick fingers over
his close-cropped, dark hair. But the smile faded quickly, and
his eyes narrowed. "I should have never doubted you, Henry."
For a moment, Henry thought he sensed something in Owen's
voice, but he decided it must be his imagination and let it go.

Henry set down his box of switches and walked across to
Owen. Still grinning, he slapped him on the back. "What say
we cook a turkey without setting the lab on fire this time," he
laughed.

Owen causally nodded. His smile was somewhat forced.
"Yes, let's try it."

For the next couple of days they used the detector to find
holes in the shielding, and the device worked like a dream.
Every day after they were finished, Henry tinkered with it,
improving it. It was almost like it was as much a project as the
oven was.

Everything went fine for about a week, and then suddenly
it all went bad. Henry and Owen were tinkering with the oven
when the detector suddenly began to scream like a fire truck,
the needles on the gauges slamming against the pegs.

Owen immediately suspected that Hansen had done
something since he was sweeping next to it, and he yelled for
him to get away. But when Henry rushed up, he confirmed it
wasn't Hansen. "It's coming from outside the lab!" he screamed
over the alarm. "Something outside the lab is broadcasting
electromagnetic radiation!" Then he was headed for the door
as fast as his old legs could carry him.

What was waiting for him outside stopped him dead still. The sky was filled with a greenish glow and an eerie hum that drowned out the sound of the alarm. A thunderstorm was building off to the north. And in the midst of all of this, less than a mile away and a few hundred yards up, a glowing disc lazily hovered, firing a beam of light into the sky.

It felt like he stood there forever, his mouth hanging open, his arms limp at his sides, staring wide-eyed into the sky. It barely registered on his shocked mind when the alarm stopped its yammering, and the hum and its progenitor faded off into the distance.

Owen came out, or maybe he'd been there all the time, and led him back inside the building. He sat him down in a chair and, from somewhere, came up with a glass of brandy. The burn seemed to bring back his senses. After the second glass, he could talk again. "Do you understand what just happened?"

Owen looked at him with narrowed eyes. "We just stepped into something we shouldn't have."

"No! No, you're wrong. We just discovered what was causing the weather problems—and discovered a way to find the people doing it. A little more work and we can make the whole thing mobile. All we need to do is get a hold of the Army and let them know what we've found out."

"Yes, no doubt the Army would be fascinated. Let's get back to work and get the thing refined down."

* * * * *

"That's pretty much all that I remember. I went home that night, went to bed, and sometime in the middle of the night they came and got me. Everything after that is pretty fuzzy, until I woke up in that motel room."

"Anything at all you can remember about the head man?"
He shook his head. "I'm sorry, Rick. I was only awake a couple of times. And he had that black hood over his face."

"It must have been Hansen that tipped them off."

"I'm sure it was. I never really trusted him. But then we didn't have anything important to worry about, so it didn't really matter."

I slumped back in the seat to digest what he'd just told me, and the next thing I knew he was shaking me awake. "Rick, we're coming into town."

I scrubbed the sleep from my red eyes and glanced out the window. I would have preferred to do this at night, but we didn't have much choice. We needed to get out of sight as soon as possible. By now they'd already found the cowboy gang at the motel. They might even be looking for this car.

The building looked a bit less ominous in the light of day. As a matter of fact, it wasn't a bad piece of property had we been in the business. An electric garage door opened into the alley, and after pushing in the service door with my shoulder, I tripped the control and Kate pulled the wagon in. I think for the first time since the motel, I felt a bit safer as the door came down. Kind of an out of sight, out of jail kind of thing.

When they climbed out of the car, I suggested we take a look at our new home. It was quite a place. The second floor must have been used as his office. It had a bank of television monitors hidden in the wall behind the desk. From there he could watch every entrance and each room in the building. Near the monitors was a row of switches that controlled all the doors. And a second row below that was used to arm the alarms everywhere in the building. The place was a virtual fortress, including a secret exit through the sewers from the lab in the subbasement.

A place this big took money and some kind of front to cover the operation. So an idea occurred to me as we finished our tour. I kind of wanted to know who really owned this building. It might just give us a clue as to who was running the whole operation.

As we got off the elevator on the second floor in the office, I told Kate and her father what I was thinking. "Kate, your father and I are pretty much marked men here in town. But you're a relative unknown. So what I'm thinking is you could go down to the courthouse and find out who is registered as owner of this building. I've got a pretty good idea, but I'd like to know for sure."

"And what excuse would I have for asking?"

"Real estate. Act like you're an agent for some big corporation looking for a location here in town."

She looked down at her dirty khakis, torn blouse, and work boots and said, "And what makes you think I can carry that off?"

I shook my head and smiled. "You're probably right. Even though you look positively beautiful to me, you might have a little trouble convincing them. So I'd say a shopping trip is called for beforehand." I handed her a fistful of cash that I had taken off one of the thugs back at the motor court. "Spend whatever you need—they're paying for it."

She scooped the cash up out of my hand, smiled and said, "Well thank you so much, Captain Steele. I'm sure I can find something that will do the job quite nicely." Then she was gone to clean up and head out.

I got back in the elevator and rode down to the subbasement where her father was tinkering in the lab. From the way he was walking around, picking up things and admiring them, you'd have thought it was Christmas. "Whoever put this lab in the building was an electrical genius. There are things here that your brother and I only dreamed of when we were working." He picked up a piece of equipment and shook it in my face. I had to squint to see what it was. "Look at this, Rick! This is a diode, and it's no bigger than a penny. This is almost science fiction."

I had to try and bring him back to reality. "Professor, that's all really great, and someday when we've got lots of time, I'd love to have you give me the guided tour. But right now we've got a mess out there, and people are looking to kill us. I need a way to find them before they find us. Remember what they did to the girl from the diner. That could have just as easily been Kate."

He put the piece down, and his face became dark and apologetic. He ran his hand through his thinning hair. "I'm sorry, Rick. I'm an old man and I've seldom seen anything like this outside of a trade show, let alone put to use. What is it you need me to do?"

I gave him a weak smile and remembered the first time I climbed into a new jet. I knew exactly what he was feeling. "You said that out at the old lab, you put together a thingy that could find the saucers. Do you think you could do it again with the things that you've got here?"

He gazed out across the lab, and I could feel the excitement building in him again. "With what I've got here, I could come pretty close to building you an atom bomb if I had the fuel. But why?" he asked, blankly.

"We find them, we end this thing."

He walked over to one of the benches and started assembling equipment. "Sure, sure, Rick. I'll get started on it right away."

"I'll be upstairs in the office waiting for Kate and taking a closer look around if you need me."

* * * * *

It was about twenty minutes later when Kate came in with four or five shopping bags and the local paper. She tossed it on the desk, face up. She looked pretty grim. "Better take a look Rick, 'cause you're quite the celebrity."

There it was in black and white and an inch tall: "War Hero Ads Two More to His Crimes at Motor Court!" Written under that in smaller type was "Search Intensifies." And there was a picture of me from my Air Force file. I read quickly through the article. It also credited me with the killing of Hansen and his partner. In disgust, I tossed it back on the desk. That wasn't going to make it any easier to move around.

"Did you see, Rick," she called from the other room where she was changing, "they didn't mention the cowboys at all. Just the clerk and the girl."

"Yeah," I yelled back. "Nothing at all about the gunfight. They're picking robbery as the motive. At least they don't know that we've dumped the Packard."

"Or at least the paper doesn't know that," she said, swirling into the room.

If I thought she was beautiful before, this time she nearly stopped my heart. She had found a nice, gray, three-piece business suit. The skirt hugged the curve of her rear, hiding nothing and accentuating everything. Nice, sensible heels and nylons bottomed out the ensemble. And on top, she had pulled her auburn hair back into a bun, showing off her high cheek bones. Last but not least, she had picked up a pair of horn-rimmed glasses to give her a bit of a mousy, business look. But for me, the effect was just the opposite.

My breath whistled out over my teeth. "Wow! I don't know where you're supposed to work, but I want a job there."

She spun around gently on one polished toe. "Sorry Captain, we don't hire pilots. Too rowdy for our company's image."

"And just who is it you work for?"

"Whom," she corrected. "Acme Manufacturing. We build numerous items. My boss is a little black duck, and our largest client is a very wily coyote."

I laughed at the cartoon references, but the grimness of the situation crept back over my face. "Be careful, Kate. One slip and it could mean the end. If it looks like things have gotten too hot, don't hesitate to take off. Get as far away from here as you can. Then call Edwards and leave a message with Sergeant Joe Cord. If you don't come back in twenty-four hours, I'll call Joey. Got it?"

She nodded that beautiful head. "Got it. I'm going to go down and tell Dad I'm leaving. Then I'm headed downtown."

I walked over to her and took her purse from her hand. It was unusually heavy, about the same weight as that of a Colt automatic. Opening it, I pulled out the pistol and stuck it in my pants pocket. "I'll keep this until you come back. Most office girls don't carry army surplus cannons in their purses."

"And if I get in trouble?"

"Then you'll still be alive when it's over, and we'll come get you."

She stuck out her luscious, red lower lip in a fake pout, but she didn't argue anymore. She just climbed in the elevator and hit down.

CHAPTER 7

At an unknown location, the man in the black hood paced the room. Everything was coming together now, but still he was anxious and worried. With Rick Steele still alive, it could crumble in mere seconds.

The door to the room opened and one of his men caught him pacing. "You okay, Boss?"

"No," he growled. "I'm not okay, and I won't be until you tell me you know where Steele is." His eyes blazed behind the holes in his mask.

"Everybody's out looking. We'll find him. Besides, he's only one man."

"Stop and think just how much trouble that 'one man' has been to our plans already. He's forced us to move out of town, and now he has the Professor.

"As long as he's alive, we can't feel safe. We're about to begin Phase II, so he has to be found!"

As though in response to his last comment, a small bell rang somewhere behind him. "Get out! I've got things to do." The man shrugged his shoulders and turned to go back out the door. The Hood's eyes didn't leave him until the door closed. Once he was alone, he crossed the room and pushed a hidden lever, causing a section of the wall to rise. Behind the wall was a radio transmitter. With a well-practiced hand, he turned the dial and pressed down the button to speak. "Yes?"

"Report." The voice coming from the speaker was oddly accented, as if it wasn't accustomed to speaking English.

When the Hood spoke over the radio, the bravado that he had shown with his men was gone. There was almost a twinge of submission in it now; he almost cowered in fear of whomever he was speaking to. "Phase I is nearly complete. And we are ready to begin Phase II. All is going smoothly and as planned."

"And this man who was interfering, he is dead?"

"He will be very shortly," he lied, "and the Professor will once more be in my custody."

"See that this is so, or we will find another agent!" Then before the hooded man could reply, the radio went dead. He fumbled for the chair behind him and sagged into it, trembling. Quietly to himself, he said, "Soon I will have no more need for you. Then we shall see who will be replaced." Out loud he hollered through the door, "Maxwell! I need a progress report! We need to find Steele!"

* * * * *

I was downstairs in the lab helping the Professor wind something called an induction coil when Kate came back. I was glad for the excuse to stop. A plane, I could fly. A car, I could drive. But explaining what made them work was for guys like the Professor to figure out. Besides, any excuse to look at Kate was okay by me.

She was all excited with whatever it was she'd found out and was just dying to tell us. So I dragged over a couple of the stools and cleared a spot on the bench for the papers she was carrying. "So tell us what you found out."

She pushed a wisp of hair back from her face, took off her fake glasses, and started in. "Well, my first stop after I left here was the Court House. I figured that would be the best place to find out about the building. And boy was I right! The old lady that worked there was a talker and was just looking for somebody to talk to.

"I told her who I was and what I wanted, and it was like somebody had said 'go.' I heard all the history I'll ever need."

I interrupted her before she could ramble on. "Do you think you could tell us a bit of what you found out?"

A frown wrinkled that smooth forehead and brought her pencil-thin brows together. "Just what do you think I'm doing?"

"I don't know, building suspense?"

The eye glasses came hurtling towards my head, and I plucked them out of midair. Her lips hardened in a tight, thin line, and fire flashed in her blue eyes. "I should know better than to try and explain anything to a pilot! All they ever want to know is how fast will it go and is she easy!" She tossed the papers down on the bench, turned, and clacked out of the room in her heels. "You think you know so much—read it for yourself!" She slammed the door and I could hear her going up the stairs.

The Professor walked across the room while shaking his head. "Not much luck with women, I see. Otherwise you'd have known just to let her run 'til she was done." I could hear him tsking as he went back to winding his coil.

I was left sitting on a stool in the lab, wondering when it all went to hell. One minute everything was fine, and the next I was all alone, looking like a fool. "What did I do wrong, Professor? All I wanted was the information!"

He sat his coil back down on the bench and stuck his hands in the pockets of his lab coat. With a scowl putting more wrinkles in his face, he said, "She came back very excited that she had done such a good job for you. And then you belittle it by not listening to what she had to say." I started to speak, but he stopped me with a hand. "You seem to be a bit blind to the respect she has for you, Rick. My daughter is an extremely intelligent woman, yet she has been almost constantly deferring to you over everything that's been happening. No doubt she's not much like any of the women you normally deal with."

He paused for a moment, studying his shoes while he seemed to think over what he was going to say next. Then lowering his voice and watching the door, he said, "I think she's falling in love with you."

My mouth fell open and something warm started to fill my chest. And when he thought I was going to speak again, I got another look at his hand. "I know, I probably shouldn't have told you. But the situation we're in right now demands things of us that we wouldn't normally consider doing. None of us may live to see tomorrow. So I thought it was necessary."

I didn't wait for him to finish. I was out the door and up the steps, two at a time. When I crashed through the door upstairs, my breath was a burning fire in my lungs, and my heart was a trip hammer. She was standing there in her blouse and her slip. She turned towards me as I burst in. Her mouth dropped open in surprise, but before she could speak, I scooped her up into my arms and buried her lips with mine. The curve of her body melted into the curve of mine. We were joined together as one, our mouths hungry for each other. And finally, when neither of us could go any longer without a breath, our lips parted.

My mouth was inches from hers, and I said, "I'm sorry, Kate. I can be such a fool."

A smile played at the corners of her lips. "Something tells me I'm going to have to speak with that father of mine."

"He only told me what you wouldn't, and what I was too blind to see for myself." Then her lips were against mine again.

Our tongues met. I tasted the sweetness of her soul and felt the fire of her body. The room was suddenly too warm and my knees too weak. There was a feeling growing inside me that I had never felt before. And I did something that I had never done before. I pushed her away. This was not the place or the time. "When this is all over…"

I saw disappointment in her eyes—but understanding too. This room, in the midst of this war, wasn't how it should be with a woman like her. I backed up a step, my breath coming in ragged gasps and my vision blurry. I reached out for her hand, but then I pulled mine back. To touch her would simply start it all again. Reluctantly I took another step back. "I need to go back downstairs. Come down when you're done changing, and we'll go over what you learned." As I turned to go, I'm sure my feet never touched the floor.

* * * * *

Neither her father nor I said a word when she came through the door, but a blush started somewhere below her collar and spread quickly to her cheeks. I'm pretty sure that my color matched hers.

She climbed up on the stool next to her father at the bench and touched him on the leg. Something unsaid passed between them, and they both smiled. I started to speak, but the slightest movement of that hand told me it wasn't a good time. So I just closed my mouth and waited.

Kate picked up the papers from the bench and used them like a pointer to keep our attention. "The woman at the Court House said that the building was bought by the RC Ranch about six months ago for a totally outrageous amount. Then the owners brought in contractors from outside the state to remodel it. And since there aren't building standards here in town, nobody has ever been inside it. She said that after it was finished, it became quite the hub of activity, with trucks coming and going at all hours of the day and night. Then suddenly all activity ceased, and it was just a car now and again."

"Did she say anything about the other night?"

"No, and when I asked her about it, it was like nothing happened here."

"Well, maybe she lives too far away to have heard anything."

Kate shook her head. "No, I asked her about that too. She said that she lives only a block or so away. That's how she knew about the trucks coming and going."

I rubbed my hand over the stubble on my chin, and the thought that invaded my head was that I needed a shave before I kissed her again. Quickly I pushed that away and got back to the subject. As long as I kept my eyes about her shoulders, I was okay; but at the same time, I had to not look into her eyes or I was caught. "So nobody knew a thing about the other night? No gunfire? Nothing?"

She shrugged, and my eyes drifted. I pulled them back. "Not according to her. Not even a police report."

I turned my stool so I could look at her father instead of her. That helped some. "Anything else?"

She tilted her head a bit to the right, crossed her legs, and was right back into my field of vision. "There's some more about the ranch. She told me that up until just a short while before they bought the building, it was quite a going concern. One of the best dude ranches in the Southwest. Lots of tourists coming through town to play cowboy. Then it all dried up. It had been city slickers that were coming to town, but instead it became hard men—the kind that looked like they'd just gotten out of jail.

"At first there were some problems between them and the townspeople, but that just seemed to melt away, and everybody started getting along fine."

It didn't make any sense. A whole town that saw nothing, heard nothing, and within a short period of time, accepted criminals into their midst like one of their own. I was missing something, but I just couldn't see it. "I'm thinking that maybe I need to pay this 'ranch' a call after sundown and see about brushing up on being a cowboy."

CHAPTER 8

With Kate's map in the seat beside me, I turned the station wagon to the southwest of town and headed out. The sun was just setting, and according to her, the ranch was about twenty minutes from town. It should be good and dark by the time I got there.

For all the trouble that we were in, there was still a smile plastered across my face, and thoughts of Kate occupied my mind while I drove. This was all something more than I had ever dreamed of—a smart, beautiful woman like her falling for a sky jockey like me? Not my usual pickup by any means. Most of the women I'd dated were as hard as the planes I flew and every bit as fast, and they were forgotten just as quickly.

Probably for the first time in recent memory, I was actually thinking about settling down, maybe even raising a family. Then a bump in the road pulled my attention back to my driving, reminding me of where I was going and why. Settling down was the last thing that I should be thinking about when I didn't even know if I'd still be around tomorrow morning.

The moon had just started to rise as I pulled off to the side of the dirt road and into a small gulley. I figured that I was about a mile from the ranch and didn't want to take the car any closer for fear of raising a dust cloud. No sense in advertising the fact that they were going to have company. Leaving the car hidden and covered with tumble weeds and mesquite branches, I set off for the house with the automatic in hand.

The country was mostly rocks, small hills, and scrub trees. Not a lot of cover, but I did my best to stay hidden behind what little there was, just in case somebody was watching. But I didn't really think they were. So far, it looked like they'd pretty much had a free rein at what they'd been doing.

I topped the last rise without incident. Keeping low with my belly in the dirt, I got my first look at the ranch. It was like a scene from a B Western—a long, low-slung bunk house, a split-rail corral, and a barn.

The main house couldn't have been more of a cliché if Rockwell himself had painted it. A front porch made out of boards, gnarled posts supporting the roof, a triangular bell, rocking chairs gently swaying in the breeze—all just like a painting. And just as silent. No cattle, no horses, not even an old, yellow dog. If this ranch had been one of the busiest dude ranches in the Southwest, it wasn't anymore. And where had the animals gone?

I lay there in the dirt waiting for the clouds to part before I moved. I could barely make out what looked like raised mounds of dirt in the corral. The clouds shifted, but the feeble moonlight didn't help. So finally, gun first, I started my crawl across the corral. My intentions were to use what I thought were mounds of dirt for cover.

But they weren't dirt, they were horses! Dead horses that had starved to death, bloated now and filled with maggots. Biting my tongue to stop from puking, I rolled quickly away from the corpses and went through a frenzy of trying to get imaginary bugs off me. Finally I got a hold of myself and started across the corral again, this time avoiding the humps.

When I reached the side of the barn, I climbed to my feet, my back hugging the wall as I made my way to the sliding door. It moved easily as I pushed it back just enough to get a look inside. The smell told me what waited inside, but the coast appeared to be clear. So taking a deep breath, I moved it open a little further and stepped in. The stench of death in the confinement of the barn was almost overwhelming. I flicked on my flashlight and swung the beam around. Cattle and horses lay scattered around the barn where they had fallen, all in various stages of decomposition.

In the center aisle a flatbed truck sat, its unknown load covered with a tarp. In front of it, a late model Lincoln was parked. There was so much road dust covering it that it was hard to tell what color it was, but my hand fixed that. A quick swipe and the blue showed through. Lower down on the bumper were the bite marks the Packard had left, and the rear window was missing. There wasn't much doubt now. I was at the right place.

It was the truck that intrigued me the most though. It was about the same size as the one that had left the marks on the floor of the garage, and whatever it was carrying was causing it to squat a bit on its springs. I moved back from the Lincoln and towards the truck.

Someone had covered the rear wood with diamond steel plating and added tie-downs for the ropes that held the tarp. I was about to hoist myself up onto the flatbed to investigate that tarp when something that looked like a fist but was the size of a bucket hit me in the side of the head, and I decided to take a nap instead.

Dimly through a haze, I heard voices in a language I couldn't understand. My best guess was that they were talking about what to do with me, and I hoped that one of the words I kept hearing wasn't "maim," "dismember," or "kill." Then they must have made a decision, and I felt a hand grab the back of my belt and lift me off the floor. Whoever they were, they were incredibly strong, because he carried me outside like a piece of luggage. I kind of faded in and out as we crossed to the house, catching just enough conversation to know that the strong guy and I weren't alone and that somebody wasn't real happy. I passed out again as we went through the door and into the house.

The next thing I knew, they were slamming my butt down hard in a chair, and I felt them tying my wrists as I faded out again. Then suddenly I was swimming for my life through a lukewarm river. Sputtering and gasping for air, I fought my way to the surface and forced my eyes open. I wasn't anywhere near the water. I was still tied to the chair, and somebody had just dumped a bucket of putrid-smelling water over me.

I blinked to focus my eyes. Then I blinked again to make sure that I was awake. I was in what appeared to be a den or a study—steer horns on the walls, stuffed animals, Indian blankets. It was pretty much what I had expected since I first saw the ranch.

It was the man behind the desk that made me blink. He was dressed like a gambler—dark suit, string tie. Could have been from any number of Westerns, all except for the black hood that covered his face. He was fingering through the things from my pockets when he heard me sputter back to life.

He pushed my things into a pile on the desk and picked up my gun. He slid the clip out, and he tossed it and the gun with the rest of the stuff. Then he looked up, and our eyes met; or at least my eyes and the red glow coming from his mask met. "At last, Mr. Steele, we meet. I must admit I am surprised that one man could be so much trouble. Our operation was running quite smoothly 'til you came to town." His voice was low and gravelly, almost like he was covering his real voice.

"You should have thought of that before you killed my brother!"

He paused for a moment, and then he nodded. "Yes, maybe blowing up the lab wasn't the wisest of plans, but it seemed necessary at the time. Had I known how you felt about him, I might have reconsidered."

As I felt some of my strength returning, I put pressure against the ropes that held my wrists to the chair. "Escape is impossible, Mr. Steele. Even if you were to break loose from the ropes, my two companions would quickly overpower you."

I had sensed someone behind me, but I couldn't twist my head far enough to see who it was. Most likely it was the two men that brought me in. I struggled in the chair just to convince myself he hadn't been lying.

He stood up and walked around the desk. The rest of his outfit matched the top half—black leather gloves, high-heeled boots and spurs with black corded pants. As he crossed in front of me, his right fist lashed out and made my head rock. I knew now why he was wearing the gloves.

"You've been wasting my time, Mr. Steele. Valuable time. Tell me where the Professor is and I'll make your death a swift one." I couldn't see, but I could hear the smug look on his face. "A death, I might add, that has been a long time coming!"

"After all, 'Black Bart,' what's one more death to a man like you?" The fist lanced out again. This time it caught me on the other side of the face, and I felt the blood from my lip run down my chin.

There was fury in his voice when he spoke this time, and both his fists were clenched. "I regret each and every death, but they were necessary!"

Tied like I was, I did my best to shrug. "Can't conquer the world without breaking a few eggs, right? Just ask old Uncle Adolph or maybe one of his pals. They all felt the same way."

Suddenly he was in front of me, his hands clutching my jacket and his face inches away from me. The smell of his aftershave as it violated my nostrils reminding me of something. There was a hiss in his voice when he spoke, and

I was glad he was wearing the hood, or I'd have been covered in spit. "You stupid fool! You're just like all the rest! Can't you see I'm trying to save the world?" He pushed me violently. The chair went over backwards, and I whacked my head on the floor. All I could see through the blur were two pairs of cowboy boots, about size fifteen, standing behind me. One set came forward, and the giant they were connected to grabbed my chair and set it back up right. He had fringe on his shirt and red hair sticking out from under his ten gallon hat.

"I think he said that once or twice too. It's a new decade. Time for new, more inventive ideas, don't ya think?"

He slammed his fist down on the desk, and my things bounced. "Since the end of World War II, Mr. Steele, this country and much of the world has been on the wrong track. Nuclear weapons, the balance of power, the rise of the Communist party—all these things are tearing the world apart. My benefactors and I intend to remedy that."

"By killing everybody with the weather?"

"No, I intend to do it by showing them a new way to think. A new understanding. A completely new way to live! Unfortunately, the weather disruption is a necessary step in the process. Without it, Phase II wouldn't be possible." The timbre of his voice had risen, and he was almost preaching. "It is time that they learned that war is not the answer! And if they won't listen, I'll make them listen!"

I ran my tongue over my swelling lips, wishing I had a free hand to wipe the blood away. The vision in my left eye was getting a bit squinty, but I knew that I could hold out probably longer than he could. Besides, it gave me a little more time for a plan. Now if I could just think of one.

"And just how do you intend to do that? Larry and Shemp back there?" I toss my head back in their direction.

There was some chatter behind me in that language again, but he silenced then with a slice of his hand. "In a way. The Slingari have given me something that will make the people think just the way I want them to. You can see how well it's worked here in town."

I shook my head and sucked on my sore lip. "So that's why everybody around here is so oblivious to what's happening— some sort of mind control!"

"Yes. A formula that leaves the people completely able to function but open to my suggestions." He sighed beneath his hood and leaned down on the desk, supporting himself on his outstretched arms. "You are trying my patience, Steele. If you're waiting for a rescue, it's not coming. As I told you before, there's no escape. I will find the Professor with or without your help. So just make it easy on yourself and tell me where he is."

One squinty eye and a fat lip made it hard to make my face look like I was thinking it over. It probably just looked like I was in pain. I waited a couple of breaths and said, "You know, you're probably right. You could find him on your own. So…"

I had him. All his attention was on my face, and I hoped Larry and Shemp weren't smart enough to see it coming. He walked around the desk and got close, waiting for my answer. One step, two, and then I let him have it—both feet right in the gut. Next time, they'd tie a guy's feet too.

He went down with a whoosh and a moan, and my chair shot over backwards again. As he lay there moaning, I felt pretty good, at least until one of those giant cowboy boots caught me in the side. I felt the toe of his boot turn my ribs into an accordion.

As my world went all swirly for a second, he pulled himself to his feet and leaned against the desk to catch his breath. "Burn it," he gasped, "burn it all! Everything—the ranch house and him with it!"

CHAPTER 9

The teletype chattered again. These days, every time something came through, it was bad news and meant another emergency bulletin that the world would probably never hear. He pulled the paper from the machine and walked across the lunchroom to show it to Phil, his producer. Empty cardboard cups and overflowed ashtrays littered the table. And Phil's face was starting to resemble the table. The long days and nights without sleep or even access to the outside world were starting to show on both of them. They had stopped being able to smell each other long ago. Behind them and outside the window, another bank of dark clouds began to roll in.

Phil read the bulletin and handed it back. "Do we go in with a special or wait for the hour?" Tom asked.

Phil shrugged his boney shoulders inside his sweat- and coffee-stained shirt. "I don't really think protocol exists anymore, so do whatever you want. Nobody's gonna listen anyway."

Bob raised his eyebrows, admitting that his boss was probably right. But just in case, and because he had to do something or he'd go crazy sitting around, he started for the booth. Before he went in, he flipped all the switches and turned up all the dials. They could handle a bit of empty air for a couple of seconds. Then he was in his chair. "This is radio station QRT on the air with a special bulletin. Please stand by." He gave his imaginary audience time to gather around the radio before he continued. "Federal authorities have warned that water supplies throughout the Midwest have been determined unsafe to drink. They recommend boiling and extreme conservation. I repeat. Until further notice, water supplies are unsafe to drink. Boiling is recommended, and limit intake as much as possible.

"In related news, federal troops, due to the conditions of the roads and swollen rivers, are unable to reach some of the areas with major damage. Stay tuned for more bulletins as they happen." He flicked off his microphone and leaned back in his chair to light a cigarette. At least the machine down the hall was full, so they weren't going to run out of smokes any time soon.

* * * * *

General Travis climbed out of his jeep and into the knee-deep mud. The second storm of the morning was forming up, and the river was over a mile wider that it had been ten minutes ago. He slogged forward towards the water's edge where a handful of army engineers were studying the situation. "Damnit Lieutenant, what's going on? We can't sit here with our butts hanging out in the rain all day!"

The lieutenant took off his helmet and wiped the rain from his face with his handkerchief. "Sir, we sent scouts both up and down river looking for a way across, but it's almost impossible. Every time it looks like it might slow down, another storm hits and it just gets worse. It's almost like it's intentional."

"Don't give me superstition, Lieutenant! Give me answers! What about the Air Force?"

He shook his head, making drops fly. "Nowhere to land, sir. And even if there was, the weather is keeping everything grounded." Lightning cut across the sky, and thunder chased it, emphasizing his opinion.

"I don't care how, but find me a way across that river!" he growled. Then he slogged his way back to his jeep. Climbing in, he ordered his driver to pull back to high ground, and he set up a command post to wait out the weather.

* * * * *

I lay there on the floor, tied to the chair, facing the desk. I watched as the Hood's booted feet left. Behind me I could hear Larry and Shemp moving around, just out of my range of vision. One of them went and then came back again. There was a splash of liquid, and the smell of kerosene began to fill the room.

I struggled against the ropes, but this wasn't the movies. They'd done way too good a job of tying me. One of the red-haired, fake cowboys came around front and made a big show lighting a match. A grin split his face, giving me a peek at crooked, pointed, yellow teeth. He tossed the lit match in the kerosene, and there was a loud whoosh as it caught. "Now you die," he gargled in his strange accent. "Finally!"

I heard a noise from behind me like a squirrel in a vise, and I figured it was his partner laughing. I was truly glad that my impending death could cause them so much amusement. Then the door slammed and they were gone. Over the rapidly rising roar and crackle of the fire, I could hear the Lincoln and the truck start up and drive off.

Smoke was filling the room, and I could feel the heat against my back. I knew that if I didn't move, and move quickly, Mrs. Steele's favorite boy was going to be way too well done. I was lying on my right side with only my hands tied to the chair arms. Using my left leg and a little momentum, kind of kicking and swinging it, I managed to roll the chair over and myself onto my knees. Once on my knees, I was able to slowly stand and kind of crabwalk to the desk where my stuff was piled. Then, leaning across and using my tongue and chin, I pushed my pocket knife to the edge where I could pick it up.

Very slowly I eased the chair back until I could feel the front legs touch the floor, and then I rocked back until it was sitting up. Once again, I was glad I'd been taught to keep my knife well-oiled. A flick of my wrist flipped it open, and I started sawing away at the rope. Until I got the hang of it, I cut more wrist than rope.

A fit of coughing racked my body. I forced my eyes open to try and see what I was doing, but between the tears and the smoke, it was mostly by feel—or without feeling, in my case. Blood from the cuts made my hand slick, and I nearly dropped the knife. It didn't help that my hand was nearly numb from being tied so long. Coughing and crying, I felt the strands of rope part, and my hand was free!

But there wasn't time to celebrate; the fire was all around me now. The leather on my jacket was smoking, and the flames were licking at the edge of the desk. They had reached the open beams in the ceiling, and the roof was catching. I quickly cut the other wrist free. I felt my knees pop as I stood, and using my arms like a basket, I scooped up the rest of my life off the desk and clutched it to my chest. It's amazing what you focus on when you're about to die.

There was a wall of flame between me and the door, so all I could do was try and save what little oxygen was left in my lungs and run as fast as I could through the fire. I knew the door would be useless, so I propelled myself forward and off the floor. I heard rather than felt the glass of the window shatter and the frame part. The sudden rush of air into the fire was like an explosion, and I was blown clear, flying the rest of the way onto the porch.

I climbed weakly to my feet and plunged into the horse trough by the hitching rail. I know it was only seconds, but it seemed like I was under water for hours. The same putrid water they had dumped on me earlier was a godsend now. I sputtered back to the top as the roof of the house caved in, sending a shower of sparks over me. I crawled out of the trough and moved away to take stock.

Hands and face felt like second-degree burns. My eyebrows were gone, and my hair was a knot of tight, singed curls. The jacket and heavy khaki pants had probably saved me some damage, but even so, they were in pretty bad shape. Lungs were full of smoke. Felt like I might have a cracked rib or two where Shemp hit me, so breathing was something I was thinking about giving up. One eye was swollen shut, and my lip was puffy and bloody. And to top it all off, as I limped down the lane towards the car, I was wishing that I had parked closer.

I don't know how many times I fell down. Each time I did, it got harder to get back up. In the delirious state that I was using for consciousness, I was on the verge of panic. The desert seemed to go on forever, and I had just about convinced myself that I had done such a great job of hiding the car that I had already passed it. Twice I stopped and turned to go back, but a wacky little voice told me no, and I forced my feet forward again. Plod, plod, fall, get up, plod. My mouth was hanging open, and my tongue was swollen from the fire and from the energy I was expending. My boots were full of sand and were grinding against my feet. Every couple of steps I'd cough, and pain would rack my chest. Plod, plod, cough, fall, plod. Like a zombie, I kept moving.

Then I saw the car, or at least I hoped it was the car. Mirages don't happen at night, do they? I tried to remember. All I could remember was Mrs. Wilson in front of the class trying to teach us multiplication tables. I was thirty-five, sitting at my desk all burned and broken, and she was telling me five times five is twenty-five and that the capitol of Nebraska is Lincoln. *Damnit, woman! Can't you see that I need to know about mirages at night?* I screamed. She just smiled and went on with the lesson.

I staggered out of my seat to force the answer from her, and I crashed into something big and shiny and covered in branches. I pushed away from it to go around, cursing whoever had put it there, when a bit of sanity returned, and then I realize I had put it there and that it was the station wagon.

With the last of my strength, I pulled open the back door, picked up the water bag, and fell onto the back seat. I pulled out the plug and let the tepid water run over my head and into my mouth. It was the most beautiful thing I had ever tasted.

It was a long time before I roused myself again. I felt a little better. Oh yeah, I was still in major pain, but I had a modicum of strength back. I crawled, or more like fell, over the seat and back into the driver's seat. I stepped on the starter, but all it did was whirl; then I remembered I had to turn the key on. I did and repeated the process. This time I heard the engine roar to life. I slipped it into to gear, and trailing branches and tumble weeds, I took off for town.

CHAPTER 10

The drive back to town was a nightmare. I kept slipping in and out of consciousness. Luckily for me, the road was pretty much empty of traffic, and I could straddle the center line to stay on the pavement. Every breath I drew over my swollen, torn lips started a fire deep in my lungs and set off a fit of coughing that left me even more breathless. The taste of blood filled the back of my throat, and my one remaining eye gave me a pirate's view of the world. It's a good thing my hearing was still intact, because it was the only thing that saved me from becoming a bug on the front of a truck. At the sound of his horn, I jerked the wheel back to the right and over onto my side of the pavement. Barely escaping the crushing force, I could feel the hot breath of his exhaust as he flew by me. I sat panting on the side of the road until the panic passed, and then I pushed down on the accelerator again.

Hunched over the wheel like I was, I must have looked a bit like Quasimodo driving the wagon as I drew closer to town. I tried to stay on the side streets and away from the police. It wouldn't do to get arrested now, not after all I'd had to do to get this far.

At last the building slid into my narrow field of vision, and gratefully I pulled up to the door and honked my horn twice. The automatic opener lifted the door and I drove inside. I could hear a scraping sound from the passenger side of the car and guessed that I had gotten too close to the side of the door.

I didn't have enough energy left to care. I barely had enough to push down on the break and turn off the key. As the engine died, so did I. My head fell forward and somebody somewhere started to honk a horn at me.

I felt somebody pull back on my shoulders, and the honking finally stopped. With a Herculean effort I pushed open my eye and saw Kate with a horrified look on her face, trying to get me out of the car. My swollen lips attempted a smile, and I said, "Hi Honey, I'm home. But I think I scratched the car on the garage door." Then I was gone.

* * * * *

The lights flickered and then died, leaving the station silent and cloaked in shadows. Across the room Phil flicked on a flashlight, its beam picking Bob out of the darkness. "Well, there goes the generator. It's either under water or it finally ran out of fuel."

"Had to happen sooner or later. What do we do now?"

Phil shrugged his shoulders, making the light dance a bit. "I don't know. I'd kind of hoped the Army would've gotten here before this happened. So I guess we're on our own."

Bob stood up, put on his jacket, and pulled on the skirt to straighten out the wrinkles. "I guess then we take a look at what the rest of the world looks like."

Outside, the lightning ripped across the sky and the thunder rumbled. Inside, Phil trembled a bit. He reached into the pocket of his jacket and laid a small revolver down on the table.

"Where'd you get that?" Bob asked.

"It's been in my desk drawer since we had all that trouble with those street punks."

"What are you going to do with it?"

"Haven't really decided yet. Always kept it there in case things got out of hand. Kind of out of hand now, don't you think?"

Bob shrugged and reached inside his jacket for his cigarettes. He shook one out for Phil and one for himself. "What say we have a cigarette before we decide?"

Phil nodded his agreement and settled back into the chair. With both of their cigarettes going, he flicked out the light, and only the glowing tips showed that they were there.

* * * * *

Boats! Of all the stupid ideas. He was supposed to load his troops into *boats?* What did they think he was—the Navy? The infantry travel by foot and wheel. When they need to cross a river, they build a bridge. They did not rely on a boat. The general shook his head, making raindrops fly off his helmet, and walked towards the shoreline, still cursing under his breath. A group of inflatables sat waiting for him and his troops. He climbed over the side and into the nearest one. As he did, he called to his aide. "Have the men break up into squads and try to get as many as possible into each boat. I'll take a contingent with me and set up a command post on the other side. Make sure everybody wears a life vest. Dead soldiers won't do me or those people out there any good!"

The corporal nodded and set off across the soggy ground to get the troops ready for transport.

General Travis gingerly walked to the back of the boat and stared out across the raging river. It seemed to go on forever, with trees and other debris racing by in the current. Overhead, the cloud cover kept the pewter-colored sky at a perpetual twilight, broken up by the flashes of lightning. White caps topped the river. "How far is it, Sergeant?"

"Estimate's at about five miles across, sir, and growing all the time." Looking out across the river, he added, "It's not going to be a Sunday jaunt, sir. Below the surface it's full of snags and other garbage, and it just keeps shifting. Even the same path every time won't guarantee a safe trip twice in a row."

The general laid his hand on the sergeant's shoulder. "You'll do alright, my boy. I know you will."

The sergeant's back seemed to grow a little stiffer. "Thank you, sir. Better get them loaded."

With the troops on board, numbering about twenty men plus the general and the pilot, he backed the boat out into the current. Immediately it began to buck and roll against the waves. The general watched the faces of his men, all combat hardened veterans, go from the white of apprehension to the green of motion sickness as the boat pitched and yawed. The general squatted low and clutched the strap, even his own stomach reeling a bit.

For a few feet they would make headway, then a wave would hit them, and the back of the boat would rise up and out of the water. The engine roared to match the wind as the pilot fought to bring it back under control. Then it would all crash down again, the men tumbling about with only their straps saving them from being pitched overboard. Branches, dead animals, and other debris raced past them as they cut across the current.

They had covered nearly half the distance to the other shore when disaster struck. The pilot had just straightened the boat once more when suddenly, like a leviathan from the deep, the remains of a farmhouse rose from under them. The peak of the roof caught the boat, forcing one side up and nearly flipping it over in the air. Soldiers tumbled out and into the dark water where they disappeared almost as suddenly as they hit. They bobbed back to the surface and were swept away downstream.

At last, the boat pulled away from the main channel into calmer waters that were still roiling, but were without the great waves and surprises. The general—his helmet long gone, soaked to the skin, hair plastered to his head—pulled himself to his knees in the boat. "How many gone?" he yelled above the roar of the outboard.

There was a moment of hesitation, and then somebody called from the front of the boat, "Five, sir, and most of our gear."

"Just be grateful you're alive, son. Before this is over, I'm afraid a lot more boys won't be."

The pilot ran the boat up onto the shore, and the general, suddenly very old, made his way to the bow to disembark.

* * * * *

I had been running for hours. No matter where I ran, no matter how fast, and no matter where I hid, they always found me. The two aliens, Shemp and Larry, were always there to drag me back and pin me down again. I could hear the man in the hood laughing, his voice rumbling like thunder, and raindrops of fire were falling in a deluge! And all around me was an overpowering scent, like…

Suddenly I couldn't breathe—there was something over my face! I tore at it with hands that had no fingers. Had they cut off my fingers? How would I pick my nose? How would I use an elevator? I hurled it away from me. A scream of rage rose in my chest. Suddenly, I was falling!

I landed on the floor with a thump, and to add insult to injury, the small oxygen bottle rolled off the couch and landed on top of me. I lay there, covered in sweat, weak as a newborn, and tried to gather my wits. I was in the upstairs office on the floor in my underwear. My hands were bandaged like cheap mittens, and there were strips of adhesive around my chest, holding it together. And I was starving.

Slowly my poor, depleted head began to focus once more, and the world started to make sense. I remembered what had happened at the ranch, the drive back here, and Kate and the Professor getting me out of the station wagon. After that, it was pretty fuzzy. I had been drifting in and out of consciousness… the two of them bringing me upstairs and undressing me… Kate bandaging up my burns…taping up my broken ribs. After that, there were only the nightmares.

I slid the bottle off my chest and slowly sat up. The room swirled and dipped, but then as I waited with my eyes closed, the world stopped jumping around and the stars behind my eyes went away.

Slowly I rolled to my right, and holding on to the couch for support, I worked to get my knees under me. Every motion was agony. I made the first step and settled my butt down onto the couch. Then, an inch at a time, my "mittens" clutching the arm of the sofa for support, I made the supreme effort and rose to my feet.

I made it! A smile crossed my cracked and dried lips. Then just as quickly, my arms were windmilling in the air, looking for anything to grab onto, and I was falling again!

At least this time I landed with my butt on the couch. Gripping the arm and the back with my mitten-like hands, I pulled myself up once more. I took a deep breath, waited for the room to stop spinning, and then very slowly started to wobble my way to the desk. I was about halfway there when the elevator doors opened, and Kate rushed out.

"You idiot! Are you trying to kill yourself? You should be lying down!" She rushed to my side and stuck her head and shoulder under my arm to help hold me up.

I tried to smile. "Well, I just didn't feel like sleeping anymore. Every time I closed my eyes, they just popped back open all by themselves!" She helped me around the desk, and as a wave of dizziness hit, I sat, or rather fell, into the chair. "Stop the room, would you? I want to get off."

She shook her beautiful head. "That's probably the morphine. It should wear off shortly."

"Morphine?" I felt my eyes pop like a cartoon. "Where did we get morphine?"

She cleared some of the papers off the edge of the desk and sat down. Reaching out, she felt my forehead. "The same place we got the bandages, and the penicillin, and the burn salve, and the rest of the stuff. I got it at the drug store."

My mouth matched my eyes. "You went and bought this stuff at the drug store? Why not just hang out a sign that says, 'here we are'?"

She shook her head again. "I didn't buy it. Dad and I broke in during the middle of the night and stole it. He bypassed the alarm, and I broke in and got what we needed. The way you were when you showed up, if we hadn't, you'd probably be dead."

I'd have shaken my head if I could've without it falling off. Instead I just gave her a lopsided grin and watched the sparkle dance in her eyes. "Doctor Kate Gallagher, you are truly amazing. Want to tell me how bad I am? And how long was I out?"

"You were unconscious for six days. Cracked ribs, first and second degree burns on your hands and face, bruises, contusions. Pretty much what you'd have gotten if you had stepped out in front of a freight train."

"A freight train named Larry and Shemp, with a guy in a hood as the engineer." I told her what happened at the ranch and watched the horror cloud her face.

"And you walked away from that?"

"I'm not real sure that 'walked' is the right word. But needless to say, I did get away. What about the country? How bad is it?"

She got up from the desk and walked across the room with that slight sway in her walk that only the most beautiful women have. She pulled a pan out of the cupboard and set it down on a hot plate. "I'll tell you about the rest when I get some soup in you."

"You steal the hot plate too?"

"NO!" she retorted. "Dad made it up with some stuff from downstairs. Helps to have a genius for a father, rather than a jet jockey! Now sit there quiet until I get your soup done."

CHAPTER 11

With two cans of Campbell's in me, I was feeling a little better. I settled back into the chair to listen to the news. The Professor had come up while I was eating, and he was pretty anxious to share what he knew. Things up north hadn't gotten any better while I was out. Because of the high water and fierce storms, even the Army was having trouble moving. And now they'd found that the water was radioactive and none of it was safe to drink. "And Great Southwestern Water has volunteered to truck water north."

Suddenly, I knew. The fog in my befuddled brain began to burn off, and I knew! I slammed my bandaged hand down on the desk in triumph. Then I wished I hadn't. I tried to shake away the pain but that only hurt more. Finally I just laid my hand back on the desk. Across from me, Kate and her father looked at me like I was crazy. "It's all really simple," I explained. "They used the weather to mess up the water supply. Who would suspect? And then they show up with fresh water tainted with whatever chemicals they're using for mind control, and nobody's ever the wiser. Hell, they've even got the Army involved now, so they'll have control of a couple of battalions of troops when they're done. If we don't stop them before they deliver the water, we'll never stop them."

"But we need to find them first."

I looked at the Professor, and he gave me that absent-minded look, like he really had no idea what I was talking about. Very slowly I said, "Professor, I need to know—is the detector done?"

He took off his glasses and began polishing them, and so faint that I barely heard him, he said, "Nearly."

I felt what was left of my eyebrows coming together. "Nearly? Is that like nearly ten minutes from now, or like nearly ten days from now?"

He hesitated and scratched his mostly gray head. "Just a bit more work and some fine tuning."

I took a deep breath and held it, trying not to lose my temper. "We may have to go without the fine tuning." I turned to Kate, hoping for better answers. "Exactly when did the radio say they were going to head north with the water?"

"In three days they hope to be loaded and ready to roll."

"There's your deadline, Professor. You've got two days. If we don't find them before they leave…" I didn't feel that I needed to finish. "Please get it done." As he got up and walked to the elevator to go back to work, I turned back to Kate.

"I need you to go through all the paperwork you got from the county. We need to find where they could be hiding, just in case your father can't help us. More than likely, they're holed up in a property that either RC Ranches or Russell Carlson owns."

She nodded as I got up from the desk and started peeling the gauze mittens from my hands. The skin underneath was red and raw, but I needed my fingers. "I need a pair of soft, leather gloves, Kate."

She walked across the room to a pile of clothes on a table. She tossed me a pair of gloves from the top of the pile. "I'm way ahead of you, cowboy. Gloves, new pants, new shirt, new boots. They even had one of those old, ugly fedora hats you like so well." The hat floated across the room and I caught it.

I tried it on, but it felt funny, and when I took it back off and ran my hand over my head…"What the hell happened to my hair?"

Kate bit down on her ruby lips to stop from laughing. "When you showed up downstairs, most of it was gone, and what was left was just singed fuzz. So we had no choice but to cut it off. It'll grow back, so don't worry."

* * * * *

Half an hour later, showered, shaved, and dressed in new clothes, I felt like a new man. Or at least I felt like an old man in new clothes, but I was ready to go again. When I came back into the office, Kate was at the desk going through the paperwork. I walked over and sat my butt down on the corner. With the thumb and first finger of my right hand, I lifted her chin up until her blue eyes met mine. "Thank you, Kate."

A blush crawled up her cheeks. "For what?"

"You know I wouldn't have made it without you. You were the anchor that brought me back here, and you were the one that nursed me back to life."

This time she did grin. "Hey, I had to save you. After all, who else is going to save the world?"

I climbed off the desk, shaking my head as I made my way to the elevator. When I looked back, she was watching me go. Then the doors on the elevator closed, and I was gone.

As the doors to the elevator opened into the lab, I wondered if I was in the right place. It looked like a hurricane had gone through it. Half-finished parts were strewn about the room, piled on nearly every flat surface as though they were waiting for some genius to come along and finish them. I felt a bad feeling rising deep in my gut. Then I saw it.

The "it" in question covered most of the eight foot table, with two Tesla coils on one end, a jumble of wires, a control board, and what looked like an oscilloscope attached to it. The Professor's electromagnetism detector was about to be born.

I stopped suddenly in my trek around it. He was following so close, he bumped into me. "Well, will it work?" I asked.

With his upper lip curled under his lower as he thought about it, he finally nodded. "It's not quite as pretty as the one your brother helped me assemble. And I don't have his skill in transistors and diodes, so I had to do everything the long way. That's why it looks so big and bulky." He pushed some hanging wires back up on the bench just to illustrate his point. Then using his glasses as a pointer, he continued. "My last problem was finding enough power to charge the Tesla coils. I finally figured out that the power from the elevator was enough."

To demonstrate, he pulled down the switch on the elevator, and I heard it grind to a halt. Faintly I could hear pounding coming from inside. Kate must have been on her way down when it shut it off.

* * * * *

The flatbed truck was pulled up the mountain as far as it could go without falling off the other side. The tail was hanging off into space, and the tires had stopped just at the edge.

Two men dressed in coveralls climbed out of the cab and began untying the ropes that were holding down the tarp. As they pulled it off, their precious cargo was revealed.

It looked like an antiaircraft gun smashed into Buck Rogers' disintegrator: A long barrel composed of five cylinders, side by side, surrounding a smaller barrel in the center. All attached to a triangular swivel mount with a large blast shield in the rear.

Behind the blast shield, a mass of electrical dials, gauges, and switches. And two large handles that were meant to rest on a man's shoulders while he was firing it.

The man on the passenger side removed a large box from under the gun and strung the attached cable down to the ground. The box also had switches and gauges. He took a pair of earphones like those that airline crews use and settled them over his ears. When he was done, he flipped the switches across the front of the box. Then he nodded to the other man.

The second man had donned his own earphones and climbed up onto the back of the truck. He fiddled almost endlessly with the dials on the back of the "gun." Then he began flipping switches of his own. When each new switch clicked into position, a barrel of the gun began to glow. The first was red, then green, bright yellow, blue, and lastly purple. As the glow grew brighter, a deep whine rose from inside the machine. Both men put dark glasses over their eyes, and the man on the truck hit the last of his switches. The whine became earsplitting. A beam leaped from the front of the gun and pulsed its way up into the clouds.

* * * * *

The sky above the swamped Iowa farmlands began to boil. Clouds formed from nothing and within instants coalesced into a black, rolling mass, broken by bolts of lightning cutting across its surface. Suddenly the clouds split, and nature's most deadly fury was born. Like a giant, probing finger, the tornado flicked out of the clouds, tested the ground, and leaped back up. Then it tested again. Seemingly satisfied with what it found, it unleashed its full fury. Moments later, a twin was born, then a triplet! Trees, houses, and the very ground itself was torn from the face of the earth as the three sisters moved across the horizon.

Behind the storms, there was only emptiness. Ground as barren as the face of the moon was all that was left, and it was being drowned with drenching rain. Amidst the rising waters were the bodies, torn from what they had thought were safe shelters. What had once been a farmer lay face down in the mud, horribly twisted. A few feet away from him, a female that might have been his wife lay broken and mutilated by the wind, her out swept arm almost seeming to reach for him. A mile away, two little girls lay arm in arm, as peaceful as if they had just gone to sleep, but dead none the less.

The storm reached out across miles, through the town and through the temporary base set up by the soldiers. The only signs that they were ever there were the bits of scattered equipment left behind.

The storm took the giant concrete and steel elevators filled with grain and tore them to shreds, scattering their contents across the land.

The first tornado hit the school, tearing off the roof. The second hit, sucking out the children. The third wiped the building from the ground. Everywhere they passed, it was the same. They tore through the gas station, ripping the pumps from the ground and causing the spark that turned the corner into a fireball. Houses, businesses, churches—everything fell. Nothing withstood their fury! If it wasn't for the bodies and the debris scattered about, it would have been the earth a million years ago.

* * * * *

The general saw the rapidly approaching storm and tried to call to his men above the rising wind. "Cover! Take whatever cover you can find! Stay low to the ground!" He had grown up here in the Midwest, so he knew what one of these storms could do. But they were facing three!

He ran down the hill towards the remains of the highway. There the ditch was only partially filled with water. The wind tore at his clothes and threatened to toss him backwards. He crouched low as he ran, urging others ahead of him. "The ditch! Go to the ditch, men!" As they reached the edge of the ditch, the others hesitated. A quick glance towards the west told him they were out of time, and without a second thought, he plunged face first into the cold, murky water. Holding his breath, he covered his head with his arms and burrowed down into the mud for cover. One minute he was drowning in the dirty water, and the next it was gone—sucked out from around him and right out of the ditch! He felt the suction and scrambled for something to grab on to, but there was nothing but grass. Like an iron filing to a magnet, he was torn from the ground and felt himself flying backward into the sky. For the first time in his life, he screamed!

CHAPTER 12

I was about to tell him that I thought Kate was in the elevator when a klaxon began to sound. I put my hands over my ears to shut it out and yelled, "What the hell is that?"

The Professor grinned and covered his own ears. "I added a larger alarm so we could hear it anywhere in the building."

They could hear it in Denver. "Can you pinpoint where the attacks are coming from?

He pointed to the lines jumping across the scope. "By measuring the height of the stroke, it'll give us an approximate distance from town."

"I don't care how it works, Professor. I just need to know where they are! And could you shut off that damn noise?"

He flipped a switch, and either the room grew suddenly quiet, or I had gone deaf. Then, pushing a bunch of stuff off one of the benches, he spread out a road map. "The machine shows about fifteen miles west of town. And figuring that they would want the highest place that they could find," he traced across the map with a dirty nail on a stubby finger, "I would put them right about here—at Spirit Mesa."

I clutched at his shoulder in urgency. "Can I make it? Can I get there in time?

For half a second he thought about it, his bushy brows knotting into a furry line across his forehead, and then he nodded. "Their bombardments usually last about an hour. And once you get close, you should be able to see them. You've got time!"

The instant he shut down the detector, I heard the elevator restart and finish its trip down. Kate emerged with fire in her eyes, but she quickly cooled as I told her what was going on. She'd brought down my gun and my new hat with her. She handed them over. "I figured you'd be going someplace, and I thought you might need these."

I shrugged into the shoulder holster and put my jacket back on. Looking at her, I couldn't remember when she had looked more beautiful, or concerned. Gently I reached out and touched her cheek, wishing that my gloves weren't in the way. "I'll be back. If they were going to manage to kill me, they'd of done it by now!"

"I don't suppose I can go with you?" A little pout played at the corners of her beautiful mouth.

I plopped the hat on my head and kissed her. She started to pull back in surprise and then melted against me. "We're going to talk about that when I come back," I said, meaning the kiss. Then I turned for the elevator and didn't look back again.

* * * * *

In the old days, before settlers corrupted the West, the Indians had named the peak Spirit Mesa. It was the highest spot locally, and the place where their ancestors ascended to heaven. As I approached it now, you would have thought they were all going at once from the glow!

I parked the wagon in the rocks at the bottom of the hill and started the long climb to the top. I figured now that I was here, one way or another I was going to be able to follow them back to their headquarters. I tried to move as carefully as possible and not kick up too much of the prairie dust, but I might as well have not cared. I don't think the two men at the top could see much other than the glow anyway. But it was the screech that really tore into me. I could ignore the glow by looking away, but the whine was tearing my head apart.

As I crouched down behind a rock, I felt rather than really heard the whine begin to lesson. Between the gun and the Professor's alarm, I wondered if I'd ever really be able to hear again. Carefully I looked around the rock.

The man with the gun braced on his shoulders was flipping switches, and along with the dying whine, the glow also began to fade. He locked the mount down, walked over to the side of the truck, and sat down, his long legs dangling. It was my old pals Shemp and Larry from the ranch. As I watched, Larry unplugged the box on the ground and rolled up the cable, sticking both under the cover of the "weather gun."

Whatever they were saying to each other was in their own language, so it sounded like gibberish to me. Larry pulled the tarp from the weeds, handed it up to Shemp, and climbed up to help him tie it down.

When they were done, Shemp leaped down and pulled a pack of cigarettes from his pocket. He held them up for Larry, laughed something in his own language, stuck one in his mouth, and started to chew it up.

Whatever it was that he said, Larry must have agreed, because he did the same thing.

I waited patiently behind the rocks as they picked up the rest of their things and finally climbed into the truck. When the engine growled to life and they started to roll down the hill, I made my move. Just as they rolled past me I reached out and grabbed the back of the truck, pulling myself up onto the bed. Then I quickly scrambled up and under the tarp.

It was hot under the tarp, and it smelled like they had kept it in the barn full of dead animals—which was where I'd seen the truck last. And whichever one was driving wasn't very good at it. The first corner nearly threw me off the truck. I rapidly learned that I'd better hold on if I was going to get where they were going.

The ride seemed to go on forever. Between the heat, the smell, and the bouncing ride, I was starting to feel sick. I lifted the side of the tarp to get a little fresh air, but the wind blowing between the tarp and the truck bed only made the smell worse. I laid my cheek down against the diamond plate to stop my head from spinning and hoped that I'd live long enough to get even with them for this ride.

Finally, just when I was sure that I was either going to die or at the very least puke out the lining of my stomach, the truck slowed, and I felt a change in the temperature of the air outside. Somehow it had grown cooler. I put my mouth down to the edge of the tarp and breathed deep. The air was clean and sweet with a hint of dampness, and I felt the summersaults in my stomach slow. As they did, my mind started working again. I must be underground. I could taste just a hint of dirt and mold in the air.

I heard the two of them get out of the truck, jabbering in their language. Their voices receded until they were finally gone altogether. I waited a couple more minutes and then I looked out.

I was right. The truck was underground and inside a domed kind of grotto—maybe an old mine. But if it was, it was the largest that I had ever seen. Along with the flatbed that I was on, there were two tanker trucks parked here also.

I leaped down from the back of the truck for a better look around and had to grab the truck bed to stop from falling. I stood there with my eyes scrunched shut, waiting for the room to stop spinning. Finally it settled down, and I opened my eyes again.

I was in some kind of old mine, but the roof had been raised to almost thirty feet above me, creating a grotto effect with numerous tunnels leading off on the sides. The walls had been pushed back to make the room nearly sixty feet across. Over along one wall, there were four giant copper vats like the ones used to brew beer. Great pumps and motors sat on top of the vats.

From the pumps, pipes ran over to long, fat, black hoses that hung on huge reels above the two trucks. Against the other wall, benches and tables were filled with beakers and lab equipment. All of it lit by hundreds of hanging lights so brightly that hardly a shadow existed.

My eyes must have been saucer shaped as I looked around. It was almost unbelievable the lengths they had gone to here under the desert, even down to having a central cooling system installed. But my unguided tour came to a quick end with a growl from behind me in the alien language. I turned to find Shemp pointing one of the alien weapons at me. "You are incredibly hard to make dead," he said in his stilted English.

I stepped away from the truck and spread my legs for balance, in case an opening came for me to move. "It's not just me. It's all humans. We're very hard to 'make dead,'" I answered.

He said something in his own language, and Larry, the shorter of the two, came out from behind him. And when I say shorter, I mean he was still half a head or better taller than me. He came over, ran his hands over me, found the automatic and quickly relieved me of it. Then he stepped back, covering me with my own gun.

This was the first chance that I had to take a really good look at either one of them. The last time I saw them, they were trying to make toast out of me. It was hard to judge their ages. In human terms they looked about mid-thirties, but for all I knew, they could be a million or just infants. Both had coarse, red hair that stuck out from under their caps and from time to time seemed to move of its own violation.

Long, hawk-like noses, crooked down on the end, separated their reversely slanted, cold, yellow eyes. Their lips were thick and set in a permanent sneer, like they smelled something bad; they never let their lips completely meet. And Larry had a long scar that reached from the corner of his mouth up to his eye, pulling the puckered flesh back even more. Their skin was a jaundiced color just slightly lighter than their eyes. All in all, they were the ugliest people I'd ever seen. If the man in the hood was one of them, I knew why he wore the hood! He'd probably looked in a mirror once.

Larry's pointed tongue kept flicking out over his fat lips, and I could hear his breath passing over his yellow, pointy teeth. He clicked the hammer back on the .45 just to let me know who was in charge and stepped around behind me to keep an eye on me.

Shemp smiled a scary grin. His teeth were even more pointed and yellowed. "The Kardoc will be smiley that we have found you, now that you are not dead. We will be rewarded for it." I took for granted the word "Kardoc" must have meant boss. He took his gun and waved it at his partner. "Get *saling* and make him tied tightly. We take him to Kardoc."

As Larry went off to find whatever a "saling" was to tie me up, I decided to play a bit with Shemp and see just how smart he was. With a friendly smile, I spread my arms and turned in a circle. "So tell me Shemp, what is this place?"

He must have thought the name was a term of friendship. He smiled back and waved his gun at the room. "These make you our slaves and let us win your planet. Maybe if you not be dead, I let you be mine."

That answered my question perfectly. This is where they put together the mind control drug. Then they'd loaded it into the tankers and mixed it with the water they were sending north. "So have you used any yet, Shemp?"

"Only in this town. The rest very not later."

So, I was just in time. I had to figure out a way to stop them before they could ship any of this out.

Larry came back with a three-foot piece of rope in his hand, and then I knew what a "saling" was. Quite a language lesson I was getting. He poked me in the back with my gun and told me to put my hands behind me. When I didn't move fast enough, he poked me again.

Now I don't know about you, but I hate being poked. And I hate even more being poked with my own gun. So when he did it the third time, I moved.

Larry had my gun in his right hand. I spun around quickly, grabbing his wrist, and throwing all my weight forward again, I pulled him off balance. As he stumbled forward, I lifted the automatic from his surprised hand and stepped in behind him. I was just in time, because at that very second, Shemp opened fire with the alien gun and a hole appeared in the middle of Larry's chest. I put my foot into his butt and kicked his corpse towards Shemp as hard as I could, hoping to tangle him in the body while I leaped to safety behind one of the tanker trucks.

I slid headfirst into the sand under the nearest truck, snapping a wild shot off over my shoulder just to keep him ducking. Then I scrambled up on the other side and headed for the nearest branch of tunnel.

Shemp's gun burned a trail behind me, and the rear tire of the truck caught fire and exploded. Not fazed at all, he fired again and set the rest of the truck on fire.

I lay there on the floor of the tunnel, trying to catch my breath and watching the black smoke fill the dome of the room.

You could tell that they weren't used to being defied. He came around the front of the flaming truck without caution or a hint of fear. I bounced a shot off the hood of the truck through the smoke and flames, just to keep him back while I thought over my next move.

I popped off another shot and took a quick look around the tunnel where I was laying. There was a pile of crates left over from, and I'm guessing here, the previous owner, just beyond the range of light from the big room. I fired a couple of shots at Shemp to keep him honest and skittered crabwise across the floor to see what they were. As I did, his heat gun cut a couple of swaths in the tunnel ceiling, and drips of hot rock fell all around me. I hoped that he was doing the same thing I was, just trying to keep me down while he looked after either Larry or the fire.

The wooden crates had been there a long time. They were crusted with dirt and the labels were barely visible. I lit a match so I could see and brushed one of them off. I dropped the match and nearly jumped back out of the tunnel and into Shemp's arms when I saw what it said: DYNAMITE!

How old the stuff was I didn't know, but it was old. Gently I pulled the boards off one of the cases and carefully lifted out one of the sticks. The paper wrapper was dry and flakey, but other than that they were intact. I grabbed the edge of the box and started to drag it behind me as I crawled back. The boards on the end gave way, and all I ended up holding was the end of the crate. So instead, I got behind it and pushed it back towards the entrance of the tunnel, leaving trails in the dust on the time-smoothed floor.

The truck fire had burned down to just a cloud of sooty, black smoke, nearly filling the big room and seeping into my side tunnel. A fit of coughing hit me as the smoke filled my already damaged lungs, making my eyes water and waking a burning my chest. As I wheezed to clear it, I saw Shemp inch his way around the smoking truck. He must have heard me coughing and decided it was a perfect time to make his move.

Even after my lungs cleared, I continued to fake cough, making him think I was in trouble while I fused one of the sticks. Then, rolling to the center of the tunnel, I let her fly.

Unfortunately, old dynamite isn't the most stable explosive in the world. It has a tendency to either blow up way too soon or not go off at all. This stick kind of fell into the middle of that. It landed between me and the truck and went off with about as much force and noise as a shotgun blast. It was enough to startle Shemp, but little more than that. He kept creeping.

Quickly I fused a second stick and repeated the process. Suddenly, the tanker truck was jerked to the ceiling by a giant hand and slammed back onto the floor of the grotto. It was as though God had gotten tired of his toys. Smoke, rocks, truck parts, and dirt rolled into the tunnel, pelting me and starting another coughing fit.

When it cleared a bit, I saw Shemp laying against the far wall, his body twisted at what was a strange angle even for him. I wiped the blood from my upper lip and staggered to my feet. His gun was lying just inside the entrance, a piece of slag. I kicked it out of my way and limped across the room.

Shemp was half against the wall in a sitting position, but his legs were at almost a right angle to his body. His broad forehead was split open, and through the blood I could see bone. I got down on one knee so I could see his eyes. They were still hard and cruel, but maybe just a hint of fear played behind them. "I don't know how it is for you aliens, but for us humans we call this the end of the road. No way out, chief."

His pointed, green tongue flicked out over his cracked and torn lips. "I am but one! My people are *qaraza!*" I took for granted the word meant more that one. Probably a whole bunch. "We will bury you!"

I was going to tell him otherwise, but the light faded from his eyes, and he was gone to whatever happy hunting ground aliens go to. I kicked him once with my foot just to make sure. Then, I turned back to the room.

The dynamite had created quite a mess. It had reduced one tanker to burning scrap and blown the second one over onto its side. The weather truck had two flats on the front. The windscreen was gone and the one door was crushed. On the other side of the mine grotto, one of the large, copper vats was leaking and the others were dented. Bits and pieces of flaming debris dotted the floor.

It didn't take me more than a second to decide what I had to do. I went back inside the tunnel, picked up one of the boxes of dynamite, and brought it out. I had for a moment thought about saving both the weather machine and some of the mind control chemical. But I knew exactly what would happen once I turned it over to the government. So instead, I began piling dynamite under the vats and linking the fuses together. I was hoping that if a couple caught, they would take the rest with them. Then I tossed a couple of sticks under the truck. I picked up my hat, took a last look around, lit the fuse, and ran like hell.

The entrance of the cave was a little farther than I thought. I had just emerged when a giant hand hit me on the back and sent me rolling down the hill in cloud of dust. Moments later, two more blasts hit.

As the dust started to settle, I got up, brushed myself off, and climbed into the late Shemp and Larry's car to go and pick up the wagon. I didn't look back this time as I drove off.

CHAPTER 13

They sat silently across from each other in the darkness. The ashtray had long since given up any illusion of holding the cigarette butts filling it, and they spilled out across the tabletop. The smoke hung heavy in the air like a cloudbank. The only sound in the room was them breathing.

On the table in front of Bob lay the revolver. He hadn't moved it since taking it from his pocket. It was the gun that was the focus of the room.

Then suddenly, like a beam fired from a laser, a single ray of sunshine broke through the window and splashed onto the table. As they watched, it grew from a tiny patch to the full outline of the window. Phil pushed his chair back from the table, and after a quick glance at the gun, he got up and walked to the window. As he stood looking out, he could feel the warmth on his face, and a sob escaped from deep inside him.

Bob picked up the gun from the table, slid it back into his pocket, and walked over to the window. As he did, Phil slid down to his knees, and with his face buried in his arms on the sill, he began to cry. Outside the clouds dissipated, and blue sky filled with sunshine covered the swamped canyons of the city. The storm had broken at last!

Bob helped his longtime friend to a chair. "Wait here, Phil. I'll be right back." He pushed through the double doors and out into the hallway, then quickly took the stairs to the roof.

The sunlight was blinding as he pushed open the roof door with his shoulder and stepped out onto the tar and rock covering. He shielded his eyes with one hand and searched the roof. Finding what he was looking for, he set off across the expanse. Already the chill from the storm had left the air.

His destination was what appeared to be a railroad boxcar sitting on the roof. He pulled back the dogs and stepped inside the box. It smelled of diesel and grease and was filled with what looked like the engine from a train. Off on the far wall was a bank of valves. He closed two and opened two more. After checking to make sure that everything else was in order, he walked over to a panel on the wall. He flipped five or six switches and then thumbed a big, silver button. The giant engine began to spin, slowly at first, but then it started to pick up speed. Just when it felt like it was about to spin apart, a tremendous roar filled the tiny room and the engine sprang to life.

Bob watched and listened for a few moments to make sure that it was going to keep running, and then he stepped out and latched the door. Hand still shielding his eyes, he retraced his steps across the roof and into the stairway once more. After all the time they had spent in the darkness, the stairway was like an old friend. As he watched, the lights in the hall slowly flickered to life. On his way back downstairs, Bob made a slight detour to his office. He took the revolver from his pocket and stuck it way back in his desk drawer. Then he headed for the news room.

This time when he entered the newsroom, the lights were on and the teletype was clicking away in the corner. Phil was standing in the center of the room with his jacket straightened and a pencil behind his ear. "Where'd we get the power from?"

"Backup generator on the roof, with enough fuel to last a day. Thought that if the storm was really over, somebody should tell the world! We can run it for a while, shut it down, and then turn it back on in a couple of hours or so."

Phil nodded and smiled. "Good idea. It'll let the world know they're not alone."

* * * * *

A wave of pain tore through him, forcing him to remember that he wasn't dead. Through the morphine that they'd given him, the general pushed open his eyes and took a look around. It almost made him giggle at the thought that he was doing something they didn't want him to do.

They had found him in a tree nearly forty miles from where he started, over on the other side of the river again. His uniform was torn to shreds, and his right leg and right arm were broken, along with a few bumps and bruises. He had gotten the rest of his people into the ditch on time, and he was the only casualty. Now he lay on the stretcher in the warm sunshine, waiting for evac by helicopter. The storm had broken and started to clear while he was still in the tree.

* * * * *

I sat in the station wagon, waiting for Kate to finish her shopping. It was kind of nice not being hounded by the police anymore. When the mind control drug wore off and they came to their senses, they dropped the charges. Now almost four weeks later, things had settled down to pretty much a routine.

The detector stayed on twenty-four hours a day, and the Professor continued to refine it one piece at a time. It took up just one end of a lab table now instead of an entire room. But so far, all had been quiet.

I'd been back out to the mine a couple of times to check on it, but it didn't show any signs of tampering. Everything they had left was buried under tons of rubble.

The reports from up north said that with the weather settled down, they were beginning to rebuild. It would be a long time before they'd be back to normal, but it was a start.

I'd moved into my brother's house and was thinking about staying. I'd found an old Cub down at the airport that was cheap enough and was considering a flying service between here and one of the bigger cities. Maybe even a mail route.

Kate had mentioned once that she should get back to her dig, but she hadn't made a move yet to do so. I think we all were just waiting. We knew that they were still out there and that they weren't done yet.

I took my sunglasses off and rubbed the bridge of my nose. As I was putting them back on, I heard a commotion up the street at the hardware store. As I watched, an unbelievably tall, redheaded man ran out of the store and leaped into a waiting car. Seconds later it tore from the curb and raced off down the street.

But it wasn't alone—I was right behind them. The minute I saw him I knew that he was one of them, and I didn't wait to see what was going to happen next. I fired up the station wagon and dropped the clutch. When they pulled away, I was right there with them.

There wasn't much power in the wagon, but by the first corner I'd begun to gain a bit. The coupe was about five or six years old—the kind they called a business coupe, with two doors and a small rear seat. It was gunmetal gray, possibly a Plymouth or Dodge. I could see three heads bobbing around inside.

The streets of downtown slid quickly by, and we flew through a small residential neighborhood. I took a corner on two wheels and fought to bring the wagon back under control.

The body was playing rock-a-bye left to right, while the chassis played it right to left. As it flattened out, so did the highway, into one long, straight ribbon. I pushed it to the floor and hit the overdrive. I couldn't believe my luck; I was actually gaining on them.

Driving with my right hand, I reached under my coat and pulled my automatic out with my left, and I laid it on the seat. I wasn't sure about my plan yet, but I was willing to bet they weren't going to give up easy.

I was crouched over the wheel, gripping it with both hands, watching the distance between the two of us shorten. I think there might even have been a bit of a smile on my face at the thought of catching them. Then suddenly something slammed into me hard from behind. Looking up in my rearview mirror, I saw a car full of men right on my bumper. Even as I watched, they hit me again. Only this time the car in front was nearly on my front bumper, and I was sandwiched between the two.

I was slammed forward by the one behind, only to hit the one in front and be slammed back again. I could hear the crunch of the metal. My mouth was bleeding where I'd hit it against the steering wheel, and the car was filling with desert dust.

Both of their cars were heavier than my wagon, and I knew I couldn't take much of this. Chancing a glance sideways, I could see a small road off the highway just ahead. That's where I was going to have to make my move.

As we approached the side road, I got myself ready. I pulled the seat up as close to the wheel as I could, braced my left foot against the floor, and jerked the wheel with both hands to the right. The momentum made it like trying to turn a ship at top speed. The front tires came around, but for a tenth of a second they were at right angles to the car, and they were being pushed through the dirt. The force tried to tear the wheel from my hands. Sweat poured down my face and wet my palms, making them slippery, but I held on. Just as it started to come up on two wheels, I felt control coming back, and I knew I was going to make it.

Then they hit me again! That was more than the little Willis wagon could handle. It was already half in the air, and the force of the other car against its back quarter sent it rolling out across the country. Inside of it, I had become a living ping-pong ball. I grabbed onto the wheel as I felt it go, but there was nothing I could do to stay in the seat. All the inertia of the car was directed at me.

I was against the top, against the windscreen, under the steering wheel, and back to the top again. It must have rolled ten or fifteen times before it finally settled on its top. I was wedged between the wheel and the seat, my shoulders hanging down on one side and my feet on the other.

As I hung there, blood dripping from the bang on my head, I watched a pair of shiny shoes walk up to the car. They stopped, and their owner banged on the door. "Steele! Are you still alive?"

I recognized the voice. It was the man in the black hood. My throat was dry and my voice little more than a rasp. "Yes Hood, I'm still alive."

The feet fidgeted. "And not hurt too badly, I hope? If you were a better driver, this wouldn't have happened. I just wanted to talk to you."

In vain I struggled to break free, but I was wedged tight. "What do you want, Hood?"

He got down on his hands and knees and looked in the smashed door frame. When he spoke, the honey that was in his voice was gone. "For the last time you have interfered in my plans—with my life! When success was nearly mine, you were there to stop me! Well, not again! I intend to take from you the one thing you have come value most. I want you to suffer loss the way I have all these years." He got down to where his face was just inches from mine, so close I could smell his aftershave. I could hear the venom in his voice and almost see the bits of spit hitting the inside of his mask. "That's the only reason that you're still alive, Rickie!"

Far off now, I could hear the sounds of police sirens approaching, and that stopped him from saying anything more. He stood up, and I heard the sounds of him brushing himself off. Then he said something in the alien language, and his shoes and the other two pairs disappeared from my field of vision.

The sirens stopped, wound down, and minutes later, a couple of cop boots were standing right where the Hood had been. A cowboy hat and a big, round, red face looked in the window. "You alright, fella?"

"Yeah, I think so. Just need a hand getting out."

"Be just a second. Jimmy's coming with the pry bar." He looked back over his shoulder and said, "Here he is now," and stood up. Moments later I heard the screech of metal, and the door popped open. I wiggled myself loose and crawled out onto the sand. For a long moment I stayed right there on my hands and knees, trying to orient my brain to a world that was right side up once more. Then with their help, I climbed to my feet.

CHAPTER 14

Funny. No matter how many flowers you put in a room, the antiseptic smell just never goes away. I was sitting on the doctor's exam table putting my shirt back on when I made that observation for about the fiftieth time in the last hour. There was a new, sticky plaster on my forehead and fresh tape on my ribs. After explaining to the deputies that I was just a really lousy driver, they had cited me and brought me here. From the looks I got, I'm pretty sure they didn't believe me, but at least they didn't ask about the other two cars.

They half carried, half pushed me in past a waiting room of pregnant mothers and little boys with cut knees. It was nice to know that a guy with a ding in his head took precedence over an eight-year-old with the sniffles. One of the cops helped me up onto the table while the other took down my information. Then he shoved his pad under my nose and told me to sign. Despite a bout of dizziness, I managed to scrawl my name, and he tore off my copy. I wanted to tell him I wasn't staying for the drawing but thought the better of it.

A matronly nurse came in, looked at my head, and poked me once in the ribs, all the while clucking disapproval. I'm sure that she sniffed my breath. She was looking for the merest hint of alcohol so she could cluck at me some more. But finding none, she just nodded and said, "The doctor will be with you shortly." And she was gone.

The next time the exam room door opened, it was the genius of country medicine. He was rather plump, balding, and had a tendency to wear his glasses pushed up onto his forehead, and he was all wrapped up in a spotless, white lab coat. Looking at my paperwork, he made that same remark I'd heard a million times since I was a kid. "Too bad you're not made out of steel, Mr. Steele." I just smiled like it was the first time I'd ever heard it.

Despite his handicap in humor, he did an alright job of patching me up, and did equally well at berating me for the behavior that had gotten me in his office in the first place. This brought me back to buttoning my shirt as Kate and her father came in.

She stood in the doorway, hands on her hips, and gave me that "what have you done now" look. I almost waited for her to tap her foot and thought how much she reminded me of Hepburn.

I gave her my most sheepish grin and said, "Hi Honey. Don't be mad, but I wrecked the car."

For a long moment there was only silence. Then finally, she couldn't hold it anymore and broke into a grin, and it was alright again.

The Professor bustled in around her and came over to the table. "What happened, Rick? Was it—"

I quickly cut him off before he could say any more. "You know how my driving is, *Dad*. I was on my way back and a bit overtired, and I fell asleep at the wheel. Next thing I knew, the wagon was upside down and two nice policemen were pulling me out." Looking at Kate in the doorway as straight-faced as I could, I said, "I hope the boys weren't too scared."

Her blue eyes narrowed a bit. "No, but their sister was. Are you ready to go home?"

I glance over at the doctor. "Doc?"

He nodded, making me wonder what kept his glasses up there. "Don't see any reason why not. Just take it kind of easy for the next couple of days with those ribs. And keep an eye out for the signs of a concussion."

I picked up my hat and jacket with my shoulder holster rolled up carefully inside, and after thanking him, the three of us headed out. There was just one last stop to make—smile, thank the nurse, and leave a fresh hundred on the counter to cover the bill. She just picked it up, clucked some more, and called the next patient. I wondered what she said to her husband, if she had one.

As we got in the Professor's car, I said, "We need to head for the impound yard first. My gun's still in the wagon."

As we drove to the impound yard, I told the two of them what really happened. Well, not quite all of it. I didn't tell them about the Hood's threat. That was something for me to worry about.

The station wagon looked about like I remembered, only right side up. It was still hanging from the back of the wrecker. The top was crushed in about half a foot from the top of the doors. The driver's door was flopping loose from where they'd pried it open with the crow bar. Quickly I ducked inside and fished under the seat. Luckily the deputies had no idea that there was anything in the car, so it was right where it landed. I pulled it out, blew the dust off it, and stuck it in my belt.

Then we were back in the rusty, old Ford and were headed for the lab. Kate was half turned towards me from the front seat. "So, if we have destroyed their weather machine and the mind control drug, why are they still here?"

I mulled that over a bit before I spoke. I knew at least why the Hood was still here but not the aliens. We had pretty much messed up their plans for conquest.

* * * * *

The bridge of the saucer was a lot like that of a seagoing vessel. It sat in the dome of the ship, surrounded by translucent panels of a one-way material. The navigator sat at a console in the center on some kind of gimbals that let it turn one-hundred-eighty degrees, giving the ship neither a front nor a back and the ability to travel in any direction. Normally the bridge held a crew compliment of six, but while on the ground, it was empty—except for the man in the hood. He was staring with rapt attention at the large monitor screen. On the screen was the leader of the aliens.

Like his brethren, he had the wild, unruly, red hair. But he was balding, giving the impression he was wearing a round, yellow skullcap on the top of his head. Deep wrinkles and gray in his parchment skin testified to his vast age. And unlike the rest of his people, he was rotund with fat, and his great jowls hung almost to his chest. His pointed teeth were capped in gold, and his upside down, slanted eyes were rheumy and clouded. His tone left no doubt that he was the leader. "You have failed us! At each and every turn, you have failed us! When we came to this planet, we came specifically to you. You told us that with our weapons and the one that you would build for us, we could conquer this nation and then use this nation to conquer the rest of this dismal planet!" The rage in his voice was growing.

"None of that has happened! You have lost the weather machine and all of the mind control formula. It will take months to distill enough to do what we planned. And we still do not have Gallagher to build the power system for your weapon!"

There was a sneer beneath the hood. He raised his hands in mock supplication. "Great Lord, I am to blame for none of these failures. It was your own people who allowed this to happen." A human would have known immediately that he was making fun of the alien. "I had humans to aid me, but you forced me to use your people instead."

"My people are warriors!"

"That may be, but they are not used to dealing with human beings. Each time they had Steele within their grasps, they let him escape. And last time it cost them their lives, and us the weather machine and mind control formula."

The Hood's bluff had worked, and the alien calmed down. He stroked his fat chins with a long-fingered hand. The nails glistened crimson. "And what do you propose?"

Beneath his hood, he smiled. These aliens were such fools! "Actually, My Lord, my plan is quite simple…"

CHAPTER 15

When we returned to the lab, Kate headed upstairs. I was going to follow her but the Professor stopped me. "Can I talk to you for a moment or two downstairs, Rick?"

"Sure, Professor." I followed him down the stairs and into the lab. As always, the electromagnetism detector was on, scanning for any sign of the alien ship.

He pushed some things back on one of the benches and brought out a piece that looked something like a lamp with a series of pipes and wire coils attached. "I've been working on this for quite some time, Rick." He took off his glasses and used them to point with. Without them, his eyes were small and dark. "As a matter of fact, almost since the first time I saw the saucer. It's only been in the last week or so that I got it finished enough to show it to you."

* * * * *

The Professor and I were standing in the lab next to the electromagnetism detector when the lights blinked off the first time. Our eyes met, and at the same time we both said, "The power plant!"

We knew now what they were planning, or at least part of it. Somehow they had found out about the detector and were going to cut the power so that we couldn't follow them.

I grabbed my hat, checked the clip in my automatic, and headed for the door. The Professor was right behind me. "Is there any way that we can keep power to the detector?" I asked back over my shoulder.

A big grin stretched across the Professor's face. "Yesterday I'd have had to say no. But with my new power source, it could run for years without electricity now."

I gave him the thumbs up sign and handed him one of the guns we'd taken at the motor court. "You know how to use that, right?"

Again he grinned. "Who do you think taught Kate?"

Speaking of Kate, I hollered up to her as she was coming down the stairs. "Your father and I are headed for the power plant. In case something happens, keep an eye on the locator. We think that they're up to something bigger yet."

I tossed a couple of flashlights onto the front seat and slid behind the wheel. She came across the garage and gave me a weak smile through the window. "Be careful and keep an eye on Dad. He's a little old for all this world saving."

I smiled and tugged on the brim of my hat, pulling it snug on my naked head. "Hey, he's as safe with me as you would be!"

She shook her head. "That's a real confidence builder." Then she leaned down and called through the car. "Dad, be careful."

But he wasn't listening. He was urging me out the door even before it was fully up. "Let's, go!"

I shrugged my shoulders, threw the car into reverse, and raced backwards out the door. Once we hit the street, I ran it through the gears as fast as I could. Finally reaching third, I put the pedal to the floor with no intention of slowing down until we got to our destination.

Just as we passed the city limits, the last street light flickered out. With nothing but darkness around us, I could see the glow of the power plant ahead. I pushed harder, but eighty-five was as far as the speedometer rose. The Ford just didn't have any more.

We were less than a quarter mile away when I saw it. I slammed my foot down on the brake, sending both of us careening into the dash. "Oh my God" was all I could say, and then it was only in a whisper. The Professor's eyes got big and round behind his glasses. He took them off, polished them, then put them back on to look again. But it was still there. It was shaped like a man, but a man made out of metal. A metal man nearly twenty feet tall. And he was in the process of destroying the power plant. With every swing of his long arms, parts of the plant erupted in a shower of sparks and flame. And mingling with the explosions was a mechanical roar like that of a jet engine at full throttle. It took a moment before I realized that it was coming from its open mouth, almost like an animal's cry.

Quickly I pulled myself together and climbed out of the car. "Professor, you drive!" He slid under the wheel and restarted the car. There was a new rattle under the hood. "I want you to get around back of that thing," I instructed. "I'm going to try and take out one of its legs with the machine gun!"

I was barely in the seat and hadn't yet closed the door before he slammed the car into gear, and we were slewing off down the dirt road again.

As we came up behind it, it looked just as menacing as it had from the front. Whatever metal it was made from was glistening like silver in the remaining lights. And the roar was deafening.

The car was rolling from side to side as the Professor fought it up the dirt road, and a plume of dust reached far into the night sky. Bracing myself, I threw one leg out the window and over the sill so that I was sitting on the window. Then leaning across the top of the car, I opened fire. The trail of bullets arced

126

TERROR FROM ABOVE

off into the night towards the giant robot—and they went straight through! Not one of the thirty or forty slugs that I fired touched anything. I couldn't believe my eyes. And I'm sure my jaw was hanging open, because I could taste the exhaust and the dust.

I fired again with the same result. And then I started watching. With every swing of his long arms, fire and smoke erupted and destruction ensued, but they never seemed to actually touch anything. Even his feet seemed to float just above the ground!

I slid back inside and yelled for the Professor to head straight for it. He looked at me like I was insane, but he ducked closer to the wheel and pushed the car straight ahead.

Fifty feet…twenty-five feet…ten feet. I'm sure that we both had our eyes scrunched shut, waiting for the crash. But it never came. As I opened my eyes, the car drove right through the robot. "It's a fake! Just some kind of projection!" The Professor looked at me, his eyes matching what I'm sure mine looked like—wide with disbelief. "But the destruction?"

"Over there, Professor!" I had spotted one of the aliens running ahead of the robot, throwing some kind of grenade. There was another one on the other side doing the same thing.

Aiming as carefully as I could, I fired at the Slingari on my side of the car. Even leaning out the window, the .45 was like an explosion in the car. But it was worth it. I watched him take a little leap in the air, go limp, and then fall to the ground.

Almost as though he could read my mind, the Professor cranked the wheel tight and brought the car around so I could get a bead on the other one. He tried to dodge, but my gun roared again and he slumped into the dirt.

The man of science brought the car to a halt, and I jumped out. This close I could see the projection beam coming from the weeds. I rushed over and after a quick search, found the switch, and the giant faded away. With him went the roar, leaving the night eerily silent. Then I walked over and checked the two aliens. Both were done.

Now that the robot was gone, the men from the power plant began to emerge. A burley man in a tin hat and coated in coal dust was the first to reach us. He took off his hat and wiped his forehead with a grimy handkerchief. "Thanks, mister. You saved our lives! What was that thing?"

The rest of the crew was there now, asking the same question. "Pretty much just a great big fake. The two dead guys were the real problem. How much damage did they do?"

The foreman put his tin hat back on and looked around. Then he shook his head. "Not much, actually. Most of what they took out was backup. We can be back running by morning." His men were already starting to drag out equipment to pull the destroyed transformers loose.

All this trouble and they accomplished nothing. Why? Suddenly, it came to me like somebody whacked me in the head with a hammer. I took off for the car at a dead run, calling to the Professor. "It's Kate! This was just a distraction! They're really after Kate!"

CHAPTER 16

Even after racing the car until it was smoking and rattling, we were still too late. The sheriff and his deputy were watching an ambulance drive off into the night as we pulled up. The Professor wanted to go racing after it, but I stopped him. "Wait. Let's see what happened."

As I got out of the car, the sheriff came over. He took off his cowboy hat and started drying the band inside with one of those big, blue handkerchiefs. "Should have knowed the minute I saw them redheaded fellers that you'd be involved." He put the hat back on and spit tobacco juice into the dirt, dangerously close to my foot. I tried to ignore it. Even under his own control he was pretty much the same ass.

"What happened, Sheriff?"

"Well, according to the witnesses—that couple standing over there," he indicated to a girl that looked like a hooker and a ranch hand on the other side of the street, "though they're not as reliable as I'd like—a truck full of those redheads pulled up. They jumped out, blew up the door, and started a gun fight!

"That's about the time my officer Mac got here. That was him in the meat wagon." He tossed his thumb back over his shoulder in the direction the ambulance took. "Got three of 'em before they finally got him. Don't know if he's gonna make it or not."

"And my daughter?" the Professor asked.

"She put up one heck of a fight, Professor. Killed a couple more of 'em. But it wasn't enough. They grabbed her and took her with 'em." He spit again and wiped the dribble off his chin with the kerchief. "Now, it's my turn. You wanna tell me just what's going on?"

I nodded. "Why don't you go on inside, Professor. I'll take care of this and be right behind you." As I watched him walk away, his shoulders slumped in fear and defeat, and I wondered how much more of this he could handle. He held up pretty good so far, but the worst was yet to come. And only I knew how much danger Kate was really in. That train of thought would drive me crazy if I kept it up. So I shook my head to clear it and told the sheriff what had happened earlier today.

* * * * *

The two aliens had her by the upper arms and were dragging her, her feet barely touching the floor. Her hair was wild and her clothes torn and dirty. She was like a tiger in their hands, squirming, fighting, and cursing. They seemed not to mind at all. As a matter of fact, it was like they couldn't understand English.

They came to the end of the short corridor, and with a hiss the door slid back into the wall. The aliens half carried, half dragged her onto the bridge. When they reached the feet of the hooded man, they tossed her down.

Kate landed one hip down, her arms out straight, palms against the shiny, cold metal of the floor, and her auburn tresses covering her face. Only the sounds of her breathing and sobs broke the silence of the room.

Then suddenly like lightning, she moved. Her knees came up under her, and she went to hurl herself up off the floor and at the hooded man. But the aliens were quick too. She'd gotten one foot under her and was tensing for the jump when a blow on the back from one of them sent her sprawling back to the floor. To make sure she didn't try it again, he stuck his booted foot in her back, forcing her breasts flat against the floor. The Hood walked over and knelt down on one knee next to her head. "I was going to welcome you, Miss Gallagher. But I see you are offended by my hospitality."

Through her gritted teeth, Kate muttered something he couldn't make out. "What's that, Miss Gallagher?" He leaned his head closer.

"It's DOCTOR Gallagher, you ass! Not MISS!" she spit.

He stood up and brushed imaginary dust off his trousers. "As yes, I apologize. I had forgotten all those stories of all those digs." Then to the two redheads he said, with venom showing in his voice, "Take her down and put her in a holding cell. We will need her until we get a hold of her father."

As they picked her up she began to struggle again, nearly kicking the hooded man. "You'll never get your hands on my father! Rick will see to that!"

As they reached the door, he stopped them. He walked over, took her face in his hand, and turned it towards him. "Ah yes, the illustrious Captain Steele. He won't have much choice now that I have you."

Summoning all her courage, Kate spit in his face. He slapped her with the back of his hand. "Like father, like daughter! Get her out of here before I kill her now."

As the door hissed shut behind them, he tried to contain his rage. No sense in losing it all now when he was this close. Soon he would have them all in his hands! A laugh erupted from under the hood.

* * * * * *

It took longer with the sheriff than I planned, but in the end we had come to kind of a compromise again. We both knew that the chances of help from the government were pretty slim. And like all the times before, the dead aliens were gone. Minutes after they'd been killed, their bodies had just gone up in a puff of smoke and turned to dust. So we were still on our own, but at least now we were working together. He was even going to have an unmarked cruiser delivered to take the place of the Ford. It was mine to use as long as none of the townspeople got hurt and I kept him in the loop. I agreed, or at least close enough to satisfy him. Then he and his deputy climbed into their car and roared off in the same direction as the ambulance. And I went inside.

It had been quite a fight. The garage door was lying in a pile of twisted metal, some of the frame still attached. Empty shell casings littered the floor and the air was still thick with gun smoke. I pushed my way through the debris and over to the steps.

Kate had made another stand here. There were a couple of the dark marks the dead aliens left, and the walls were pocked with bullets. When I got to the lab, the door hanging on one hinge, the Professor was sitting in a chair with his head in his hands, the room lit by a single lantern. As I entered, he looked up. "What are we going to do, Rick? They've got my Kate." He took off his glasses and began to polish them. I could tell that he was close to the breaking point and that I needed to bring him back—and quickly. "Professor, they won't hurt her as long as they still want you. Now what about that power system for the EM detector? If they make a move, we're going to need to see it."

Thank God for short attention spans. I saw lights come back on behind his eyes. It's not that he didn't care what happened to Kate, it's just that there was something else to occupy his mind. He wandered over to the bench and began moving things around, absently talking to himself. "If I shift the second phase into the third and go with the smaller Tesla coil, I should be able to triple…"

As his voice trailed off, so did I. I didn't need to stand there and watch him work. I climbed slowly up the steps and settled down on the top one to survey the damage to the garage. Actually, I just wanted to be alone to try and figure out for myself just what was really going on.

It all started with the Professor and my brother spotting the aliens' flying saucer and accidentally coming up with a way of tracking them. When the aliens found out, they killed my brother Owen and kidnapped the Professor. Then they drugged the water supply and took control of the town. All the while they were using their weather disrupter to destroy most of the Midwest so that they could drug the water supplies. And from there, on to Washington.

I don't know how long I sat there trying to figure it out, but I must have fallen asleep. I was dreaming about Owen and me when we were about ten and eleven. We were playing in the backyard and had gotten into it over something stupid, like all kids.

I pushed him, and he fell backwards into the sandbox. He rolled over onto his stomach before he got back up. I couldn't see his face, but I was sure that he was crying. I was taunting him about being a baby.

Suddenly he came up out of the sandbox and smacked me with a left hook that sat me right down and made my eyes water. When I looked up, Owen was standing there laughing—but it wasn't Owen! It was the man in the black hood. He was standing there with his hands on his hips, laughing at me! The laugh got louder and louder until it became a ringing in my ears. Then I realized it was the phone.

I shook my head to clear it and ran downstairs. There was only one person who had this number. When I picked it up, his voice confirmed it. "Hello, Steele. I have your girlfriend. And if either of you ever wants to see her again, you'll listen very carefully and follow my instructions to the letter."

My anger boiled over. "If you've so much as harmed—"

"I suggest you drop the macho attitude and listen. I'm only going to say this once. If you make a mistake, she dies!"

"Alright, Hood. I'm listening."

"I want the Professor to drive three miles west of town to the dead mesquite trees. Park the car and wait. My people will come and get him. And *he* had better come alone. If my people see anyone, they have been told to radio back. I will not hesitate to kill the girl.

"In order to assure no trickery by you, Steele, I want you to stand in the garage door where you can be seen. My people will be watching!" All that was left was the exact directions. Then the line went dead. As I hung up the receiver, I noticed that the Professor was standing right behind me.

"Is she okay? Is Kate alright? Did you talk to her?" He was pretty close to that edge again. His hair was standing on end from running his hands through it. His glasses were spotted with bits of solder and smears of dirt, his eyes wide and wild-looking behind them. He grabbed my upper arms and dug his fingers in. "I have to know, Rick. Is she alright? She's all I've got!"

I pried his fingers from my arms as gently as I could. "She's alright, Professor. I didn't get to talk to her, but she's alright. For some reason they want your cooperation, so they're not going to hurt her for now."

"What do you mean 'for now'?"

I could have lied to the old man, but what good would it have done. "The Hood is going to use her to get what he wants. And if that means hurting her to force you to do his bidding, he will. So you'd best be prepared for what could happen."

I was scared for Kate too, but if I was going to save her, I needed a safe way to follow the Professor. I avoided his eyes, looking down at the floor, and rubbed my hand across the stubble of my hair. "I need a way to follow you without being seen, Professor, but I can't leave here. For the first time in a long time, not my fists or my gun can get me out this one. I think I'm about to fail you both." I suddenly realized I'd been watching him for signs of breaking down but hadn't spent much time looking in the mirror. I was getting pretty close to the edge myself. I'd seen it before, back during the wars. A man flies so many missions without letting up, and then you find him sitting in the barracks or maybe the cockpit of his plane in tears. Doesn't make any difference how brave or how strong you are, it just happens. When it does, you're done.

But it wasn't sneaking up on me. I was fully aware of what was going on, and I was going to fight back. I spun around to face the Professor. "There isn't a way I can track you with the EM detector, is there?"

He stroked his chin and ended by pinching his lower lip between his thumb and forefinger while he thought. "Actually, I've been kind of thinking about an idea along those lines. If I had something that could emit a steady pulse, and I readjusted the detector to a wider spectrum..."

"How long would that take, Professor?"

He shrugged his boney shoulders. "Thirty minutes."

I checked my watch. "Can you do it in twenty? That's all we've got."

"I guess we'll see." And his white coat retreated into the lab. Seconds later he reemerged and took the flashlight from my hand. "Sorry. Can't work in the dark you know." All I could do was smile. I would never understand exactly how his mind worked.

Nineteen minutes later he called me into the lab. He was standing at the focal point of the two flashlights, and he was holding a flat bar wrapped with copper wire, just a little smaller than a Fig Newton. "Tra-la!"

"I think you mean 'Ta-da,' Professor."

He screwed up his face and shrugged. "Well, whatever the sound effect is supposed to be, here it is. Range is about one hundred miles and should run for about forty-six or -seven hours." He flipped something on it that I couldn't see, and the detector began making a very rapid clicking noise. I was glad he'd disconnected the alarm. "It can be used as a range finder and a locator. The screen will follow the same way it did with the saucers and the weather machine. And if it were portable, the clicks would grow faster the closer you got."

I'm sure my jaw was lying against my chest. "That's amazing! Now where are you going to put it so that they can't find it?"

By way of answer, he tucked it into his mouth and swallowed. And swallowed again. Then one more time. It went down kind of hard. His voice was a little raspy when he spoke. "If I'd have had a bit more time, I'd have made it a bit smaller." He shook his upper body like a man with a chill and swallowed again. "And made it taste better," he said as an afterthought.

CHAPTER 17

On the bridge of the saucer, the black Hood clicked off the communication device and spun his chair around to face the six Slingari standing behind him. At the sight of them, he shook his head. They were dressed in B Western outfits. "To blend in with the locals," they told him. Maybe if Tom Mix happened to stop by. He sighed and got to the business at hand. "I want two of you to pick up the Professor and one of you to watch the garage to make sure Steele stays there." And to the fourth one he said, "You I want to blow up the garage and kill Steele. Understand?" Four cowboy hats with scraggly, red hair sticking out bounced up and down.

The Hood rose from his chair and crossed the bridge. As he reached the door, he paused. "Do not fail me. If you do, you will all die in Steele's place!" Then the door closed and cut them off from his vision. Quickly he made his way to the lower decks and the holding cells.

Kate sat against the wall in a bare, eight-by-eight room. There was a force field across the door that kept her there, but it gave the impression that the door was open. She had found out quickly enough that it wasn't so. It had tossed her back across the room.

Now as the Hood approached, she climbed to her feet and came forward, being careful to maintain her distance from the door. She pushed her hair out of her face and tried to straighten the wrinkles in her torn clothes. One beautifully tanned shoulder and part of her black bra were visible through her torn blouse, and the right leg of her jeans was split nearly to the hip. "Come to torment me some more, Hood? Or did you just need another dose of really hot woman to fire you up." She ran her tongue teasingly across her lips.

Beneath his hood he smiled, immune to her charms. "Neither, Doctor Gallagher. I came to inform you that you would soon have company. Your father is on his way."

She picked up her boot and threw it at the door. There was a flash of lightning and the smell of ozone, and it came hurtling back at her like a rocket. She ducked and it bounced off the wall behind her. But she had had the satisfaction of watching the Hood jump back, despite the protective field. "If Dad's on his way, Rick's right behind him! And I'll be out of here in time for breakfast!"

"We shall see, Doctor Gallagher. We shall see."

* * * * *

I checked my watch. It was time for him to go. He took off his lab coat, put on his jacket, and we walked out to his car. The new, unmarked car the sheriff had sent was sitting behind it. The Professor gave it a quick look but then climbed into his Ford. I closed the door with both hands on the window sill. "Don't worry, sir. I'll be right behind you, and we'll get her out."

He rolled his upper lip in against his teeth and nodded. "I know, Rick." Then he turned the key, stepped down on the starter, and it clattered to life. "I just can't quite see the light at the end of the tunnel yet," he said over the engine noise.

It was my turn to shrug. I could only make promises. I slapped the roof with the palm of my hand to get him started like you would a horse and called out, "Good luck," as he rattled off in a cloud of oily smoke.

I watched until he turned the corner, then I walked back into the garage and picked up the folding chair I'd brought up from downstairs. I took it back to just the edge of the square formed by the moonlight and sat down. My position left the upper part of my body in shadow with only my legs showing, just enough to show them that I was sitting there but not enough to mess with my night vision or for me to catch a bullet.

The garage smelled of gunpowder smoke. It reminded me of the battle that Kate had fought here, and I felt my anger start to rise. But quickly I forced it back down. Now wasn't the time to lose my cool. There was too much riding on making our plan work out just the way we had it figured to go off half-cocked.

So instead, I sat there and watched the windows across the street for some sign of the redheaded clown that was watching me. It took a couple of minutes, but at last I saw just a flicker of movement. At least the Hood hadn't lied. They were really watching.

* * * * *

The Professor turned off the key, killing the engine, and let the car drift slowly to a stop amidst the grove of mesquite trees. The full moon sent shadows of trees across the ground that swayed in the wind like ghosts as he waited.

He didn't have long. Off in the distance, the dark blue Lincoln topped a dune and approached the grove, rocking from side to side. It skidded to a stop in a cloud of sand and dust just a few feet away from him. He could see that the driver and the passenger were having some kind of argument and could hear them yelling in their strange language.

As the forward motion stopped, the two passengers got out of the back seat, jerked open the front doors, and pulled out the aliens in the front seat. The one on the driver's side said something that sounded even harsher than normal in his language and slapped the driver three or four times. On the other side of the car, the other passenger from the back seat was doing pretty much the same thing. It was easy enough to guess that the two from the back were in charge. They slammed the others back into the car and walked over to the Ford.

They were dressed like rest of their people—blue jeans with rolled up cuffs, cowboy boots, checkered tablecloth shirts, and tall Stetsons pulled down so low that their ears were curled. They walked up to the car and the one in charge pulled the door open. "Howdy, Pardner! You all best be gettin' off that hoss and be comin' with us to the ranch."

The Professor rubbed his eyes and shook his head before he started to get out. Their English hadn't improved. It was, like their dress, a bad version of a Western movie.

He must have been taking a bit longer than they thought necessary because a large, yellow-fingered hand reached in and lifted him out. At the same time, his accomplice pulled out his six-gun and pointed it at him.

Barely giving him time to recover his footing, he pushed him across the sand. "I said herd them doggies now!"

The Professor staggered across the desert and climbed into the backseat of the car. They climbed in beside him, and with the other man from the front behind the wheel, they roared off into the night.

* * * * *

There are times when half an hour seems like an eternity, and this had been one of them. But I'd put the time to good use and ran through the whole thing in my mind again. There were still a few holes, but like a seed, it was starting to poke through the fertile soil that made up my mind. It wouldn't be long before I had the answers I was looking for.

I left the chair where it was and quickly went downstairs to check on the position of the Professor. Like a radar screen, it showed him as a stationary blip. Wherever they were going to take him, it looked like he was there.

Quickly I got out the map and began to plot out the coordinates. That's when I heard the noise from upstairs. I took off my boots, and in my stocking feet I quietly headed back up the stairs. As my eyes came up level with the floor like a submarine's periscope, I did a sweep of the darkened garage. I got lucky. He had been facing the wall, but as he got ready to move, he turned his face and the light reflected off his pallid complexion.

I eased my body over the edge of the stairway, staying on my belly and trying not to silhouette myself against the light of the door. I slithered towards him. He was so intent on what he was doing that I got within two feet of him. I could hear him gibbering under his breath but had no idea what he was saying. Then it didn't matter. I rose up behind where he was crouched and brought the .45 down hard against the back of his cowboy hat. The gibbering stopped, and he slumped forward into the wall.

At exactly that instant, the boys from the power plant kept their promise, and the lights flickered back to life. I thanked my stars that they hadn't been two seconds sooner, or I might be the one laying on the floor.

With the lights back on I could see what he had been doing. All around the garage, small boxes about the size of packs of cigarettes were stuck to the walls. It took only a second for me to realize what they were, and a quick search of sleeping beauty gave me the detonator. Making sure that it was off, I slid it into my pocket. Then I went around and pulled the rest of them off the walls and laid them carefully in a pile in the middle of the floor. I just might need them!

Before going back downstairs to finish plotting where the Professor was taken, I grabbed a roll of heavy wire and tied the alien's hands and feet. I was going to make sure this one wasn't going anywhere.

Minutes later, map in hand, my bag full of spare clips for the automatic and the gifts from the aliens, I climbed into the borrowed police car and set off to follow the Professor. As I pulled away from the building, I reached out and unclipped the mic from the dash and turned the radio on. "Sheriff, this is Steele. Over."

The radio filled with static, and then for a second it cleared. "Go ahead, Steele."

"I've got one of our buddies tied up in my garage, and I thought you might like to have a chat with him. He's got a bit of a dent in his forehead."

"Yeah, we'd like that. We'll be right over. You stay there until we get there."

"Sorry Sheriff, no can do. Got someplace I have to be."

"Steele, we had an agreement—" That was the last I heard because I shut the radio off. He'd never understand why I had to do this myself, and any interference would just get Kate and her dad killed. I pushed down on the accelerator and felt the big engine roar, and I raced out across the desert.

CHAPTER 18

The cool metal of the deck felt good against her bruised cheek and swollen eye. From somewhere far away, the throbbing vibrations of the engines lulled her into a dazed stupor, taking her far away from the pain. She hummed a tuneless song. Her world had grown very small in the last few hours. The Hood had come back, and while she was held by two of the aliens, he had beaten her until she had lost consciousness. That had been hours ago and only now was she starting to wake.

Outside her cell, she felt rather than heard the scuff of boots against metal and the hiss of the force field opening. Slowly she compelled her good eye to open. It gave her a slightly blurred, sideways view of the world that made her want to smile. But that made her mouth hurt. Her mind wanted to deny the truth of what her eye saw. Her father was struggling between two of the Slingari. He tore free and rushed to her side. Dropping down to his knees, he brushed her hair from her face. "Kate, I'm so sorry!"

Kate tried to speak, but the effort was more than she had strength for. It came out as only a moan.

The Hood stepped into the room and the Professor's rage exploded. He came up off the floor in a leap, a scream tearing from his throat, and his hands reaching like claws for the Hood's neck. Before he had gone more than a step, a blow to his back by one of the Slingari dropped him to the floor again. "Professor, will you never learn? We are civilized people. Can't we act like it?"

"No civilized man does this! This is the act of an animal!" he growled.

"No Professor, this is the act of a man who knows exactly what he wants and exactly how to get it." There was a cold threat of terror in his voice, and if it weren't for the hood, they could have seen his curled lips and teeth. "Her injuries are just temporary. She will recover quite completely from all of them. But if you don't do what we ask, they will quickly, and quite easily, become permanent."

The Professor raised himself into a sitting position and with the back of his hand, wiped a trickle of blood from his chin where he had hit it against the deck plating. "And just what is it you want, Hood?"

The voice behind the hood changed again. It had suddenly become sweet and light, like a favorite uncle. "Why Professor, I'm surprised at you. I would have thought you'd have it all figured out by now. I want your new, portable power source. I will give you a lab and all the equipment that you need, and you will build it for me."

Behind his thick lenses, the Professor's eyes narrowed. "And then what?"

The grin was back in his voice again. "Then I will use it to finish the job that you and Steele interrupted."

"And what about us?"

The Hood's laughter roared through the small cabin. "That is so like you, Professor. Concerned only about yourself." He laughed again. "I will release you, of course. I will have no further need of your skills."

The Professor looked longingly at Kate and nodded his concession. "I'll do what you want, Hood. Just please leave her alone."

The Hood seemed to resist the temptation to rub his hands together. "Good!" Then he turned to one of the men standing beside him. "Tell engineering to prepare for immediate take off. I want to get started as soon as possible."

The Professor's eyes grew wide with panic. They couldn't leave before Rick got there. So he tried to stall. "But what if there's equipment in my lab that I need?"

The Hood snorted and looked at his watch. "Sorry, Professor. Most likely by now your lab, and hopefully Rick Steele, are little more than dust."

"No, not Rick!" Kate moaned, which made the Hood laugh again. Then he was gone, the field hissing to life behind him. The Professor crawled across the floor and hugged Kate to him. Softly he whispered to her, "Don't worry Kate. Knowing Rick, he's on his way here right now. He'll save us."

* * * * *

The moon was playing hide and seek in the clouds, and it didn't make it any easier going across the desert without my lights. I was just about half a mile away, according to my map and my faithful, cracked compass, when I spotted the faint yellow glow over the next rise. I shut the car down and crabbed my way over the rise on my belly. I was a little surprised at what I saw. But I guess after everything else, I shouldn't have been. They had cut back into the side of a mesa like a garage. And parked in the garage, like a bloated, glowing spider, sat their saucer. It kept them hidden from detection by anything but a straight-on ground assault. I skittered my way back down the dune, and after shaking the sand out of my pants and boots, I climbed into the car and started to drive parallel from the base. When I got passed it just far enough that I knew they couldn't see me, I turned back, keeping the side of the mesa between them and me.

At about half a mile away, I stopped. I was going to have to walk from here on in. I checked my knapsack and the .45s, and I took the shotgun from the rack in the front seat and a couple of boxes of shells from the dash. The last thing I did was turn on the radio and stick the lever down on the microphone. Sooner or later they'd get tired of the static and come looking for me. But I hoped by then I'd be back and on my way to town. Then I set off across the sand.

Like I said before, the moon was pretty much a squinting eye in the sky. That had made it hard to drive, but a lot safer to walk. Without the moon and in my khakis, I was almost invisible against the sand. At this late hour, most of the desert heat was gone; and after I covered about half the distance, I wished I had a heavier jacket. I trudged my way forward, watching the glow in front of the mesa grow. The closer I got, the more I could hear the noise the space cowboys were making. It looked like they were readying for takeoff, so I'd made it just in time.

When I reached the edge of the rock, I plastered my back against it and began to edge my way around. I planned each step carefully, checking for loose rocks or anything that would give my presence away. I was pretty sure that they were too preoccupied to notice, but I wasn't taking any chances. By the time I got around to the front, I was on my belly again, doing my best to keep low as I crawled my way around.

Up close, the saucer was even more impressive than it had been in flight. It filled the cavern from side to side and to just a few feet short of the roof. The greenish-yellow glow radiated from it, filling the space with light. Two ramps were down, and on the opposite side from me, the cowboys were hauling equipment and supplies up the ramp.

I lay there, fearing to breathe and watching them load. Then, when a lull came and they were all inside, I took my chance and made my move. I leaped to my feet and ran as fast as I could up the ramp.

I was just sure that the thunderous slap of my feet or the pounding of my heart was going to betray me, but I made it inside undetected. I twisted off to the side of the door to catch my breath and plan my next move. I couldn't wait too long. The place was like a lighthouse, every wall radiating light, washing away any shadows. I took a deep breath, tossed a coin in my mind to pick the direction, and set off.

I got really lucky. The corridor was empty, and I'd gone about fifty yards when I rounded a corner and spotted a doorway with a guard in front of it. I quickly pulled back out of sight. My guess was that there weren't a lot of things worth guarding aboard a flying saucer. I reached into my knapsack for one of the rocks I'd picked up just for this, and I tossed it across the floor.

The toss was perfect. It didn't land until long after it had flown by him, and when it did, it made enough noise to wake the dead. And like any good idiot guard, he left his post and took off after the noise. I was right behind him and brought the butt of the shotgun down against the back of his scraggly, red head. There was a hollow thump and he slid to the floor. I grabbed him by the back of his tablecloth shirt and dragged him back to the door he was guarding. Good thing the floor was slick. I think they filled these boys with rocks they were so heavy! I thumbed off the force screen, pulled him inside, and nearly exploded.

I was in the right room. The Professor was sitting with his back against the wall, and he was holding Kate's head in his lap. I could see the damaged lips and the puffy, swollen eye. It opened as I came through the door, and she tried to smile. She and her father said my name at the same instant. "Rick!"

I dropped the alien and rushed over to her side. Down on one knee, I gently stroked her face. "He do this?" I asked her father, meaning the guard.

"No, he was just here to guard the door. The Hood did this to get me to cooperate."

A growl started to escape my throat. "We have to get out of here. It looks like they are readying to take off." I handed the Professor the shotgun and scooped her up into my arms.

We had gone about two steps when I heard the buzz increase to a whine, and I felt the deck shift under my feet. We were too late! The saucer was airborne once more—destination unknown!

* * * * *

Gently I sat Kate back down on her feet and helped her over to the wall. She carefully slid back down next to her father. "So what happens now, Rick?"

"Much as I hate the thought of it, I'm going to have to leave the two of you here until we land. We can't very well engage them in a shootout while we're in flight. I'll find a place to hide. and we'll wait it out." I walked over, kissed the tips of my fingers, and gently placed them on her cheek. "Don't worry, Kate. I'm not going to let anything else happen to you." Then I pulled one of the .45s from my belt and handed it to her father. "Keep this hidden and don't use it unless you absolutely have to."

He took the gun and slid it into the back of his belt. "What about the guard?"

"I'm going to dump him back in the hall, and they can try and figure out what happened. You'll both still be here, so maybe he hit his head." Then I turned and made my way for the door. As I stepped through, I reassured them it was all going to be okay. "We've beat them before and we'll do it for good this time. Trust me!" They both managed weak smiles, and I was gone.

Luckily most of this floor was storage, so it was pretty much empty of life. That gave me a chance to look around a bit. I tried the cabins on either side of the cell and both were filled with crates and supplies. I took the closer of the two, and after disconnecting the door mechanism, I settled in amongst the boxes to wait.

I laid the shotgun down on the deck beside me, pulled my knees up against my chest, and wrapped my arms around them. Even though it was warm in the compartment, a shiver ran down my spine. It seemed that the stress of all that was going on was starting to wear on me. On my way somewhere in space, responsible for the safety of the whole world, and all alone. Nothing Buck Rogers couldn't handle. Unfortunately Buck wasn't here, so it was up to me. I set my chin down on my knees and closed my eyes. Yeah, I was going to have to figure a way out of this yet. But for right now, a nap sounded like a good idea.

CHAPTER 19

According to my watch, I'd slept about four hours when the subtle shift in the gravity and a change in the engine noise told me we were nearing wherever we were headed. I unwound my body and stretched my legs.

Refreshed as I could be, and the cramps worked out, I slipped my fingers between the door and the jam and pulled it back. It slid easily and silently. When I had it back a couple of inches, I pulled out the pocket mirror from my knapsack and surveyed the corridor both ways.

The cowboy alien was back at his post in front of the door, but from the looks of him, he was hurting a bit. Then I heard the sounds of boots against the floor, and I pulled my mirror back inside. Moments later they stopped at the door, and I chanced a look. The Hood and two of his cowboys were standing there. They said nothing to the injured guard, but pushed straight ahead into the cell. I scurried back into the storage compartment and found the adjoining ventilation duct. I pulled off the grill on my side and stuck my head inside to listen.

The Hood was speaking, and in my mind I could almost see him doing his short pacing routine—a couple steps to the left, turn, and a couple steps to the right. "We will be landing soon. After the crew has disembarked, I will come and get you. We will go to meet the Delon RaChek aboard the central ship. Then on to your new quarters where you'll begin your work."

Then as the background noise of the engines changed again, he abruptly turned and left.

As soon as I was sure that they were alone, I tapped on the wall to get the Professor's attention. Moments later, he tapped back to let me know that he was listening. It was a long, slow process using Morse code, but I explained that I wanted him to go with the Hood, and that I would come after him shortly. The Professor tapped back his acknowledgement. And we were set.

I had a bit of time, so I decided to dig through the cartons here in the store room and see if there was anything that I could use. The second box was pay dirt. It contained the silvery, hooded suits that the aliens wore. And after a bit of tailoring with my knife, I looked enough like one of them to pass from a distance.

The engine whine turned to almost a deep growl, and I heard what sounded like hydraulics, which I took for the landing gear extending down. Seconds later there was a thump. The gravity got suddenly light, then heavy, and then balanced again. Against the hull there was a grinding, followed by what sounded like a giant suction cup against the side, and then a change in air pressure as the hatch opened. We were on the moon, if the Hood was to be believed.

After the sounds of the crew departed, the Hood and his two watchdogs returned. I was back in the vent, listening. He was in an almost jovial mood. "Welcome to the moon, Professor and Doctor Gallagher. I'll bet in all your lives you never expected to hear that phrase."

"Not outside of an insane asylum!" Kate retorted.

"Ah, Doctor Gallagher. Still bitter I see. You just don't realize how grand this moment is! Your being here at this time, in this place, marks a new beginning for mankind—an era that will mark the coming of paradise, free from war! Never again will mankind make war on his brothers. Quickly now, let's go get you settled in your new quarters, and then we can go see the Delon. The sooner you get started, the sooner the new world can begin."

I watched through a crack in the door as he herded them out the hatch. Once they were gone and the guard at the door with them, I figured it was time for me to do a little exploring of the ship if we were ever going to get off the moon.

I followed the corridor around to what looked like an elevator door. The two buttons on the wall, one pointing up and one pointing down, pretty much gave it away. I pushed up, the door opened, and I stepped inside. Seconds later, I stepped out onto the bridge. I don't know exactly what I expected to see outside the ship, but the view that I got from the dome wasn't it.

There were three other ships the same size as this one circling a much larger ship. They were all joined to the "mother ship" by umbilical-like tunnels. Probably what I heard attaching to the outside of the hull after we landed. All five ships nestled down in a lunar valley, shielded by mountains on all sides. Far off above the horizon, the earth looked frighteningly small and very far away.

As I studied the flight controls, a germ of an idea was starting to grow inside my feeble mind. A plan was forming to stop them once and for all. But for right now, I turned my attention to what it would take to get this bus off the ground and stopped on a block near home.

Fortunately after about an hour, the symbols on the console started to make sense, and I pretty much got the gist of how the whole thing worked. I was pretty sure that I could get it off the ground. Whether I could make it land was another matter entirely. But I could get us home.

I slipped back out of the bridge and made a quick trip through the rest of the ship, getting the general layout. My luck was still holding. I stumbled across what must have been their arsenal. Weapons were hanging on the wall, and communication devices were sitting in neat, little charging nests. I grabbed a couple of the "radios" and one of their strange pistols and stuffed them in my bag. Then I headed out for the rest of the saucers.

* * * * *

The Hood's two bodyguards led the way through the ship and into the connecting tunnel. Other than the guards, the Professor and Kate had seen very few of the Slingari; but at the far end of the tunnel aboard the larger ship, it was quite a different story. They saw guards standing at most of the doors and aliens constantly scurrying somewhere.

Nothing was said until they reached their new quarters. The Hood pressed a button on the wall and the door hissed open. He ushered them in, playing the generous host. "As I said, so much better than before."

It wasn't lavish by any means, but there were two low benches that they presumed were beds, and what appeared to be a bathroom.

"You will find suitable clothing in the closet for both of you. Get cleaned up, and I will be back in an hour to take you to see the Delon."

After the door had hissed shut behind the Hood, Kate finally broke the silence. "I guess we might as well make use of the facilities, Dad. After all, we have no idea how long we're going to be here. Ri—" She had started to say Rick's name, but her father stopped her with his hand over her mouth.

"I think you're right, Kate. After all, we should probably be *listening*," he emphasized, "to the Hood."

Kate understood and nodded. Then she walked across the room and slid open the closet. Inside were two tan jumpsuits and boots made of some unknown material. She looked at her torn clothing and at the jumpsuits again, and she forced a smile. "Not much of an improvement, but at least no holes." She took down one of the suits and headed for the bathroom. Her father stretched out on one of the benches to rest.

There was a quiet hum from the bathroom, and then a startled cry from Kate. The Professor leaped to his feet and raced to the bathroom. By the time he got there, he could hear her laughing. "Kate, are you alright?!"

Her voice was barely audible above the hum. "Yes, Dad. I'm sorry I startled you, but the shower seems to be some kind of sonic thing, and it took me by surprise. It kind of tickles. Makes your skin feel all tingly."

The professor just shook his head and walked back over to the bench. He was starting feel each and every one of his years.

* * * * *

Shortly after they had finished cleaning up, the door hissed open and the Hood returned. He walked across the room to Kate and gently brushed her hair away from her face with a finger. "Even with the bruises, still a very beautiful woman. I can understand what Steele saw in you. Maybe someday you'll realize all the truly great things I can do for you."

Kate jerked violently away from his touch, and her father came up off the bench, reaching for the gun he had concealed inside his jumpsuit. Kate's eyes were big with warning, and she shook her head. "It's okay, Dad. The Hood just took me by surprise is all." She forced a smile. "I'm not used to men I've just met making advances towards me."

The Hood snorted and gave her a mock bow. "Please forgive me if I've stepped beyond sensibilities." Then his voice hardened. "You would do well to remember, woman, who's in charge!" Then he spun on his heels and stepped out the door. "Bring them out. The Delon is waiting."

The two bodyguards came in and, with guns drawn, ushered them out the door and down the corridor.

It was just a short walk to the Delon's quarters. When the door opened and they stepped inside, it was hard for Kate to stop the gasp she felt. Never in her life had she seen such opulence. The walls were trimmed with gold and silver. Rich, luxurious carpets covered the floor. Strange paintings covered the walls, and statuaries sat on the table next to plush couches.

Across the room, which was larger than the bridge aboard the smaller ship, the Delon sat behind a desk as big as a pickup truck. And he was just as immense himself. While the other aliens had been thin, almost to the point of skinny, fat hung on him like melted wax. His jowls flowed down onto the collar of his jumpsuit, and great creases like cracks veed out from his tiny, slanted eyes. His balding scalp was the color of old tallow. And his remaining hair was like rusty straw poking out from the gold band that circled his forehead. As they entered, he rose with great effort and waddled around the desk, the wheeze of his breathing and the clank of the medals on his chest reaching across the giant room.

The Hood dropped to one knee and bowed his head. "Delon RaChek, allow me to present the eminent Professor Hugo Gallagher and his daughter, Doctor Gallagher."

The words had no sooner left the Hood's lips when there was a loud crash from above them.

* * * * *

It took me about an hour and a half to cover the rest of the ships. By the time I was done, I had a pretty good idea how they worked and had left a few small surprises for my ugly, redheaded friends. I made my way back through the tunnel and onto the central craft. I'd been pretty lucky so far; the small ships were empty of crew. They seemed to be used primarily as a power source for the big ship, so I'd been able to move unmolested. But it was going to be a different story onboard the mother ship. I just hoped my silver suit was enough to cover all but a close inspection.

After checking, I slipped quickly onto the ship and made my way to the central corridor. It was from here that I had access to all the rest of the ship. And after the time I'd spent in the other four, I was pretty sure this was the same design, just bigger. So I had a pretty good idea where I was headed.

The captain's cabin was on the second deck, just below the dome of the bridge, with private access to the bridge. I figured that's where they'd take the Professor and Kate. And if it wasn't, I was pretty sure he'd know where they were and all I'd have to do was convince him.

I was doing pretty good. The couple of times I encountered the aliens, I just kept my eyes to the floor and moved quickly away like I was on a mission, and nobody had bothered me. But as I came to the central corridor, things started to change. There were more people moving through the hallways and guards on most of the doors. It looked like the redheads were a bit paranoid.

The map in my head that I'd gotten off the wall in the engineering section said that the door I wanted was the one with two guards in front of it. Normally, I would have thought nothing of pounding two redheaded giants into paste. But somehow in a corridor filled with spectators, it just didn't seem prudent. So I restrained my basal instincts and slipped into a nearby cabin.

I stood there with my back against the door, trying to catch my breath and looking for a plan at the same time. If I were a cartoon, there'd have been a light bulb over my head. If I couldn't go through the wall, maybe I could go over it.

There was a heating register in the ceiling. Quickly I moved a chair under it and pulled the grill free. There was just enough room to squeeze my shoulders through, and up ahead a few feet I could see where it widened up into a larger duct. I pushed my pack into the square, metal highway and wiggled the rest of me in after it. There was a tense moment when my pocket caught, and I thought somebody had grabbed me, but then I realized what had happened and twisted free.

The crawl through the duct was slow and windy. Slow because I was trying to be as quiet as possible, and windy because the air flow never stopped. It felt like the interior of the duct was barely above freezing, and it was all I could do to stop my teeth from chattering. The duct was big enough that I could travel on my hands and knees. But whatever process they had used to piece it together had left razor-sharp edges at the turns. After the first couple, my hands and my knees were leaving trails.

Then I put my hand down in something wet and squishy. A quick sniff told me what it was, and I felt a tremble in my spine. What kinds of rats lived in an alien flying saucer heating duct—and how big were they? I guessed they were about the size of cats from the pile I'd stuck my hand in. That, and the eyes I could see watching me from down the duct—slanted and unblinking, fiery red, moving only when what I guessed was the nose twitched under them.

I wiggled around to where I could get to my flashlight and shone the torch down the duct. Immediately I wished I hadn't. The creature was about four feet long from pointy nose to scaly tail, which kept snapping against the duct like a whip. Completely hairless, it oozed something like sweat from the large, visible pores in its skin, giving it a wet, shiny appearance. The head was a pointed triangle of eyes, teeth, and slithering tongue.

I let my light roll to the side of the duct and pulled my knife free. The creature hunched, and then its six legs scrabbled against the smooth surface of the duct for purchase, and it leaped!

The stench was overwhelming, choking my throat and filling my eyes with tears. I thrust out my hand towards the approaching neck and felt it slide over the slick surface. I fought for a grip and managed to latch on to one of the legs. I could hear the snap of the bone, but I held fast, pushing it at arm's length to keep the snarling and snapping jaws away from my face. More than once its hot, putrid breath burned against my cheek.

I stabbed blindly with my knife. It hit flesh and I stabbed again. The creature squealed, and it began pushing against the duct to get away rather than attack. Time and time again my knife found its mark, and at last the struggle grew less and then finally stopped.

I lay there on my belly, covered in blood and slime, trying to catch my breath. God I hated this! I just wanted to go home and fly jet planes! I could feel a tear in the corner of my eye, the fault of the creature no doubt. I wiped my face on the shoulder of my suit and started to push forward again. *Don't think, Rick!*

Just act! I had to close my eyes and hold my breath as I crawled over the alien rat. And I'm almost sure my shudders made the duct rattle.

I crawled about another two hundred feet when I heard the first sound of voices, and one of them sounded very familiar. I inched my way forward to the grill and listened. "Delon RaChek, allow me to present the eminent earth scientist Professor Hugo Gallagher and his daughter, Doctor Katherine Gallagher."

It was hard from my vantage point to see what was going on. I only had a very narrow, square, view of the room below. I could see the Hood, and the Professor and Kate, but I couldn't see who he was talking to.

"I care nothing of this presenting! Has he completed his task yet? And if not, why isn't he working? And why is this hostage here? Throw the female back in her cell and put the old man back to work."

I'd heard enough. I worked my feet under me until they were over the grill and took the .45 from inside my silver suit. Then I kicked out the grill and dropped through to the floor.

CHAPTER 20

I must have been quite a sight. Silver suit covered in blood and rat ooze, gun drawn. I heard Kate scream. But my attention was on the Delon RaChek and the Hood. The Delon yelled some kind of order at me in his own language, and I whacked the fat man in the side of the head with my gun. He slid down to the floor on his oversized butt with a very audible "Oomph." As I spun to face the Hood, I realized what was wrong. With the hood up, I looked like a short, bloody alien. I quickly pulled it off and could feel a sigh of relief fill the room. Or at least parts of it. On the Hood's side, it was more like rage. "Steele!"

A grin of near-insanity split my slime-covered face, and I looked at him and said, "TA-DA!" Seeing that it was me, Kate rushed over to my side and threw her arms around my waste. "Rick! We were starting to worry that you'd been captured." She looked at my suit, smelled me, and wrinkled her nose. "What did happen?"

My grin was still holding. "I was almost lunch for some of the space wildlife! But you know me—too tough to chew." I motioned towards the Delon with my gun. "Hood, get over there with your pal so we can watch you both." The Professor had out the gun I'd given him and was covering them. And I was glad to see that he had remembered to take the safety off.

I rummaged around in my pack and handed Kate a small coil of wire and some cutters. "Tie the Hood's hands, and tie them tight."

"What about the fat boy?"

I shook my head. "No. He'll be coming back around shortly. And he's our ticket out of here, so I want his hands free. Where are the nearest guards?"

Kate indicated to the door with the roll of wire. "There are two outside the door."

RaChek was starting to come around, and I went over and pulled him to his feet. "Come on Fat Boy, time to get up!"

He pulled his fuzzy, red brows together above his milky eyes. "What is this 'Fat Boy'?"

"It is a term of deep respect on my home world." That made him smile and he stood a little straighter. "Then I shall accept this title." He straightened his uniform and pushed his chest out with dignity.

I poked his overhanging dignity with my pistol. "Don't get too pompous. It might just clog up those floppy ears, and I want you to listen to everything I'm going to tell you. If you pay real close attention, you just might survive."

He nodded his giant head. "I understand, but first a question."

I looked around the room and shrugged. "Sure, why not. What do you want to know?"

One of his fat hands came up, and I cocked the automatic; but it was just a gesture. He was a hand talker. "Who are you?"

I showed him all my teeth. "I'm Rick Steele—Super Jet Pilot, Alien Stomper, and Invincible Man." I heard the Hood snort, and I waved my gun at him. "Just ask him how many times he's failed to stop me."

"Yes, I know of you. I wish my people were as keep-going-ist as you."

I just shook my head. "We're going to walk out of here and onto the ship that we came in on, and you're going to lead the way. Any sign of trouble and you'll be the first person that I'll shoot." I turned to the Hood and showed him the barrel of my gun again. "You'll be the second." He didn't say anything, but took a quick step back.

"Delon, I need you to call in the two guards outside the door."

He walked over to his desk, pressed a button, and said something rapidly into a small speaker. The door hissed open, and the two guards entered to face the Professor's pistol and mine. "Kate, tie their hands behind their backs and find something to gag them with." I watched her move across the room. Even with her injures and dressed in an alien silver suit, she made my heart beat faster.

With the two of them tied up, we were ready to go. "You understand what I want you to do, Delon?"

His head bounced on his fat neck. "Of course! And please, call me Fat Boy!" I shook my head and started towards the door. One of us was hanging back, and I couldn't have that. I turned to him and motioned with the gun. "That means you too, Owen. You're going to pay for all that you've done."

Everybody in the room, except the Delon, stopped dead. All their eyes were big and round. "OWEN?"

I walked over and pulled the hood off his head. Despite the tasseled hair and the red eye shields, it was my brother. "I've suspected for quite some time, but that day with the car confirmed it. The aftershave and the voice when I couldn't see your face was a dead giveaway. I'd really like to know why, but I don't have the time right now." The door hissed open. I took a deep breath, held it, and the group of us stepped into the corridor.

CHAPTER 21

We made our way through the ship and almost to the connecting tunnel before we ran into any trouble. Just when we thought we were home free, somebody got suspicious and began to follow us. The communication device in my bag squawked as he called for help. I looked at RaChek and he shrugged. "He must have seen your friend's weapon. So he's calling for troops."

I took out the "radio" and handed it to him. "Call them off! Tell them he's made a mistake!"

He shook his fat head. "I am sorry Rick Steele. It is too late. The alarm has been sounded." He was right. Just at that moment, a klaxon somewhere started to ring. "Once security has been alerted, it is beyond even the power of the Delon to stop them."

I handed the Professor a slip of paper and one of the radios in my bag. "Professor, I need you to get aboard and start the engines warming. I've written down what I could make out of the startup sequence. But even so, it will be pretty much hit and miss. I don't think that Fat Boy here is going to be able keep up."

He took the paper, read what I'd written, and nodded.

Then I could hear the thunder of their approaching boots in the corridor. "Run!" I hollered. "If we can make the tunnel, we might just make it." Kate, her father, and Owen took off in the front. And Fat Boy and I got the rear. Within a couple of seconds, they were out of sight, and he was sweating and wheezing. I stopped to let him rest.

"I think I'm too robust for this. My lungs work way too hard. It gets hard to breathe."

We didn't have much time for this. "Breathe fast. We need to get a move on." I gave him a few more seconds, then I pushed him with the barrel of the alien gun. "Time to move on."

He started down the corridor as fast as he could go, but after a few feet, he stopped gasping for breath and turned blue. His fat hand reached out to steady himself, but he missed the wall and fell onto his belly. I rolled him over, but he wasn't going to go any further. His heart had given out. I wasn't real sure how I felt about that. He was leading the invasion force against Earth, yet running him to death didn't seem fair or right. The sound of approaching feet brought me back to reality, and I took off at a run. If I could just make the tunnel, I was good.

A bolt of fire took off the hood of my silver suit, and a second one scarred the wall just in front of me. I poured on an extra burst of speed and rounded the corner. The third was a little closer and cut a furrow in my shoulder, but the suit took most of it. The tunnel was in sight! Keeping low, I found the last bit of speed inside me, and I was veritably flying down the corridor. At the same time, I was fishing in my bag for a little present for my pursuer.

As I flashed through the entrance to the tunnel, I slammed my gift against the wall and ran on. I leaped through the hatch of the ship and smacked the close button. As I did, I pulled out the detonator I'd taken from the alien in the garage, dialed the same symbol that was on the explosive, and pushed the button. An instant later, the tunnel erupted in a white hot explosion that tore it from the side of the ship and trapped whatever aliens had survived in the emptiness of the moon's atmosphere.

As I climbed to my feet, I thumbed the communication device.

* * * * *

"Professor, I'm on my way to the bridge. What's the situation?"

"The engines are at about half-power and still warming, Rick. It's going to be another few minutes before they're ready for any kind of lift."

I scowled. "Is there any way you can rush it?" I was racing down the corridor and into the elevator.

"Rick, your notes were helpful, and I'm a genius, but I'm not God." I could almost see him bustling around in engineering and shaking his finger at me. "The laws of physics say it's going to take so much time to warm, and it's going to take so much time to do it."

"Do what you can Professor. I'll be on the bridge."

CHAPTER 22

As I came out on the bridge, the first thing I saw was that Owen had broken free and was standing over the fallen form of Kate on the floor. A scream tore itself from my throat, and I leaped across the room. I caught Owen in the back with a flying tackle, and we rolled from the upper flight deck down into navigation. Even as we fell, he rolled enough to bring his elbow down hard on the top of my head, making me see stars. We hit the floor together, and he tried to get his knee between us to push me away. But I grabbed the front of his jacket and slammed his head against the deck. He retaliated with a fist to the side of my head.

I was remembering all the times we had fought as kids and wondered if he was doing the same. I rolled onto my back, and he leaped onto my chest, but a quick punch to the jaw sent him reeling. I was up and in pursuit as fast as I could get my feet under me. He came up to his knees, but one of mine smacked into his chin, flipping him onto his back. I leaped to follow but froze in midair.

Owen had one of the alien pistols in his hand and was pointing it at my middle. I scrabbled for the holster on my side, but it was empty. Owen had my ray pistol, and he had the drop on me!

I wiped the blood from my lips with the back of my hand and spit on the floor. "Well brother, it looks like you've finally got your wish. But before you kill me, tell me why. Why did it all come down to this?"

Never taking his eyes or the gun off me, he got his knees under him and climbed to his feet. Leaning against the rail that separated the upper and lower bridge, he mimicked my move and wiped away the blood with his free hand. He showed me his teeth with a smile, and a strange, insane light danced behind his eyes. "I know what you're doing, Rickie. You're stalling for time. But I don't care. I've got all the time in the world." He waved his free hand towards the moon outside in a sweeping gesture. "Even now the Slingari are suiting up, and soon they'll be here to reclaim this ship."

Owen moved sideways across the bridge, and with only a quick glance, stepped backwards up the steps to the command deck. Then he walked over and settled into the pilot's chair. "Why don't you sit down too, Rickie? As a matter of fact, why don't you sit down on your hands? I'm sure we'll both feel much more comfortable that way." He might, but I knew that I wasn't going to. But he had the gun. So I settled and stuck my hands under my butt.

His grin widened, and he wiped away the fresh blood from the cut on his chin as he made himself comfortable in the chair. "Sweet Rickie, always so good at taking orders!" A cloud darkened his face, his teeth coming together and his eyes narrowing. "Especially when it was in your favor! Never cared what it was costing anyone else! Well, no more!" He seemed ready to pull the trigger, and I figured it was over. Then suddenly he was grinning again. "Remember the tree house, Rickie? And how I accidentally bumped into you and pushed you out? You were laid up that whole summer when you were ten with that broken leg." He clicked his tongue against his teeth. "No accident! I planned for weeks, waiting until you were just where I wanted you. Then BAMM!! Down you went.

"Or Boxer, your dog? When you were fourteen? He ran away? The bastard bit me! He ran away alright! I held his head under water in the creek until there was no more Boxer."

"You son of a bitch!" I spat out. All these years I had never known just how much he hated me. I thought it was just your regular sibling rivalry, not the venomous hatred he was showing me now. The light dancing behind his eyes was cold, icy. "But that's all over, isn't it? In a few minutes you'll be dead, and you'll never interfere with my life again."

I rolled my butt just a bit on the floor, and the pistol cut a groove next to me.

"Move again Rickie, and you'll never find out what you want to know."

"So tell me Owen, what's it all about? Why?"

"After we worked so hard on the bomb, I don't think we ever actually felt they'd use it. But Hiroshima and Nagasaki proved us wrong about that. Three million dead in just a matter of minutes. What had we done?

"I started my campaign then, but nobody would listen. They just took what we had done and made it bigger. And then they made more! What could I do?

"Then one night I was given a solution. One that was beyond my wildest imaginings. I was on my way home across the desert when one of the Delon's ships was on a recon mission. It passed directly over my head and then zipped out of sight.

"Then for the next year, I spent most of my time trying to contact them. I sent messages off into space in every way I could think of. Finally it all paid off, and he sent two of his people to visit me. I explained what I wanted, and they went back and informed the Delon. He must have liked my proposal, because he brought me here and we began to plan.

"He didn't have enough men or ships to tackle the United States directly, so we came up with the idea of hurting them and making the Delon and his people the saviors. That's when

I went to work on the on the electromagnetic climate control device. It was a combination of his science and my genius that created it. We put a satellite in orbit around the earth to bounce the beam off of and set up base in the Southwest. That way, no one would ever suspect where we were."

"But what about Professor Gallagher? What did you want with him?"

He grew thoughtful for a moment and the mad grin flashed again. "Even with the devastation we were causing to the food production in the Midwest, there were still weapons to be dealt with. Having dealt with atomics, I knew what needed to be done to render them unusable. I just needed a power source, and Hugo had been working on one in his spare time.

"So we blew up the lab, 'killing' me so that I could work freely and kidnap Hugo. Who would have thought that you, my darling of a brother, would come racing in to investigate my death and make a mishmash of all my plans?

"I think it's time we made sure that can never happen again. I wish I could say I'm going to miss you, little brother—but I'm not!"

As his finger tightened on the trigger of the ray pistol, a crack rang out behind him. Suddenly an odd look of surprise came over his face, and a trickle of blood welled up in the corner of his mouth. I was on my feet and across the deck before the pistol fell from his fingers. His eyes looked up at me in question, and a spot started to form on the front of his shirt. "Who?"

Kate came around the front of the chair with my still-smoking automatic dangling loosely in her hand. Her face was dark and full of rage. And there was no remorse in her voice when she said, "Me, you bastard! That's for all the people you killed and for all the pain you've caused me and my father. I told you I'd have my day!"

Owen touched the spot on his shirt and stared at the blood on his fingers. "Well, I think you've managed to kill me," he coughed, spraying tiny droplets of blood.

I pulled open his shirt, but even through the chair, the .45 slug had done way too much damage. The way the blood was welling up, there was little chance of me stopping it. I could only shake my head and agree with him.

Suddenly there was a clang on the hull outside, and a smile slowly formed on his lips. "It may not be over yet, Rickie," he gasped. "Sounds like they're coming for you."

I spun around and checked the monitors. There were Slingari all over the hull in space suits, like ants on cake at a picnic. "Damn!" I rushed over to where I had dropped my radio and scooped it up. "Hugo? How close are you?"

The communicator crackled, and then the Professor's voice came on. "Still only about two thirds power, Rick. It'll be another few moments before..." I stepped down to the pilot's station. Grasping the thrust lever, I shoved it forward as far as it would go. "Can't wait any longer, Professor! It's either now or die!"

The ship began to shudder and shake like an old man with palsy so bad that I thought it was going to come apart at the seams. Seconds ticked by like hours, and outside, the banging increased in intensity and speed.

Then suddenly it moved! Not very far, but it moved upwards. A screaming whine filled the bridge, and ever so slowly, the ship lifted. And as it lifted, it began to gain speed. Outside, the Slingari slid off and dropped to the lunar surface.

As I watched, two of the other ships began to copy my tactics. I picked up my bag and took out the black box detonator. I set the dial on the front and pushed the button home.

At first there was no sign that it had done anything. But then one of the ships began to wobble and slid back down to the moon, crashing into the mother ship. The other quickly followed suit, and silent explosions erupted over the three ships. As we pulled free of the moon, a blinding, white light tore upward from the surface, its force buffeting us like a leaf in a storm.

I could see the question in Kate's eyes. "Before I rescued you, I planted the explosives they had planned to use on me on the other ships. I was just waiting until we were clear to set them off."

CHAPTER 23

Even with all my "vast experience" at piloting flying saucers, the best I could do was to point it at the earth and hope that we hit it. After setting our course, I stepped up out of the navigation pit and walked back to Owen. With all the shaking, he had slid from the chair and was slumped on the deck in front of it.

I knelt down on one knee beside him and raised his head. His face was gray and his eyes were clouding over. He managed to force a wry smile to his lips. "Well Rickie, looks like the game is over." His voice was barely a whisper, and he spit little drops of blood on my face when his spoke. "And like always, you win again." He coughed, and the pain wracked his entire body, twisting his face. "All I ever wanted was to save the world." He coughed again, and the light faded from his eyes.

I gently laid him on the deck and stood up. As I did, I softly said, "At least one of us *did* save the world, Owen." I wiped a tear from my eye and walked over to the rail around the pit where Kate was standing. I stood beside her and watched the earth growing bigger through the dome.

Kate's hand found mine on the rail, and she squeezed it gently. "I'm sorry, Rick."

I nodded my thanks, and this time it was my turn for a wry smile. "The guy tries to kill you and take over the world, but in the end he's still your brother." I shook my head in disbelief and ran my free hand over my nearly bald skull to clear my mind.

Suddenly, the disembodied voice of the Professor filled the bridge. "Rick, are you there? Rick, do you read me?"

I walked over to the pilot's console where I'd laid the radio and picked it up again. "I'm here Professor, what's up?"

"I think we might have a problem. It looks like that full-power takeoff with a cold engine might have done some damage. Some of the gauges and controls are running in the red."

The earth was rapidly growing larger. It nearly filled the dome now. "What does it look like it's going to do?"

I could hear the hesitation in his voice before he spoke. "Probably damage to the breaking thrusters. I made a mistake and rerouted them through the main thruster when we took off, for more power. That was the second burst of power that you felt."

I sighed as the irony of the situation hit me. "So what you're telling me is that we escaped being killed on the moon just so we could be smashed into a pulp on the earth?"

"That's pretty much it," he replied.

I turned to Kate at the rail and shrugged. She gave me a weak smile in return. "So what now, Rick?"

I was really tired of saving the day here. Would kind of like to sit back in a chair and take it easy for a change. I thumbed the radio. "Nothing you can do down there, Professor?"

I could almost see him taking off his glasses and polishing them while he thought about it. "Nothing that I can't do from up there."

"Then get up here as fast as you can. I think I've got an idea."

It wasn't much, but just maybe enough to save Kate and her dad, and it might just leave me enough wiggle room to make it out of this thing alive too.

I came up out of the pit and took Kate's warm hand in mine, and we walked over to the door to meet her father. Seconds later he appeared, like always and even in the alien clothes, disheveled. "Here's my plan. There's a lifeboat station on the lower deck, and I want you two to take one as we enter the atmosphere. I checked it earlier, and it shouldn't take too much skill just to bring it down."

"But what about you, Rick?" Kate asked.

"Yes," her father echoed, "What about you?"

I smiled. I hadn't forgotten about my favorite person in all of this. "I can't let this thing come down wild. It could land in a city. So just after you two leave, I'm going to try to shut down the engines and bring it in without power. I'm hoping that the atmosphere will slow it down enough that I'll get some control and can direct it out into the desert, or the ocean, or wherever I can find."

"Chances are, Rick, that the whole thing could drop like a stone the minute you shut it down!"

"I know Professor, but I'll still have the momentum for a while, and I hope that'll keep me airborne. Now the two of you need to get below and get ready." They turned to leave, but I reached out and pulled Kate back. Even bruised, she was the most beautiful woman I had ever seen. The soft, auburn hair falling just beyond her shoulders. The blue pools of her eyes smiling back at me. There was a warmth in me I'd never felt before. Her lips were just inches from mine—so close I could feel her breath. It was warm and coming quickly, like she'd just finished a race. That spoke more to me than any words ever could. I had my hand around her upper arms, holding her. I wanted to taste her lips more than I'd ever wanted anything in my life. I pulled her closer. "Kate, I..." Suddenly the ship started to shudder as we hit the wisps of the atmosphere, and it was too late.

We were bouncing, and with our speed, the wind was screaming by the outside of the hull, making it necessary to almost yell on the bridge. I pushed her towards her father. The Professor took her arm, and they turned towards the door. "Rick..."

"Believe me, when this thing is over, I'll find you. Whatever it takes, I'll find you. Now go before you run out of time. If the buffeting gets much worse, you won't be able to launch!"

One last look and the door was hissing shut behind them. I rushed down and strapped myself into the pilot's seat. It was all the gyros could do to hold it steady; even then it was rolling like a ship in a hurricane. The light for shuttle bay number one came on, requesting launch. I hit the button, and far below me I heard a loud hiss as they left the ship. I turned the monitor control and watched the lifeboat grow small behind me.

The atmosphere was growing thicker now. It was visible as it sailed past the dome, and the temperature began to rise from the friction. I unhooked the front of my suit to try and find some cooler air.

I was watching the altimeter as it clocked off the distance, hoping that I had calculated it right after converting. The buffeting was worse now. If not for the belt, I would have been tossed from my seat. Using my landing thrusters, I forced the nose of the ship up. We were falling more like a flat rock now than a rocket. Both the meter and I were counting.

It hit my mark, and I pulled all the thrust levers back. An instant later I leaped from my seat. I literally flew across the bridge to the engineering board and sent the engines into complete shutdown. The brain of the ship screamed something at me in Slingari, but since I don't speak Slingari, I ignored it. I'm pretty sure what it said was that I was a dumb ass for what I'd just done, and it was going to kill me for it.

I lurched back across the floor and buckled myself in again. Just in time too, because the ship took a roll so big that I thought it was going to go over. But then the gyros took hold again, and it just went back to bouncing around.

I kept the landing thrusters blowing for as long as I could, using them to keep the nose up. And while that seemed to be helping, it just made me a bigger target for the friction. The temperature on the bridge continued to climb, and sweat was running off me in rivers, pooling in the lower half of my suit and in the chair.

The voice of the ship continued to scream at me over the noise of the wind, and in my anger and frustration, I yelled back, "Damnit, if you don't like what I'm doing, get out." Unfortunately it couldn't understand me any better than I it, so it was a screaming match without a winner.

If it had been a plane, at least I would have had a stick to fight like in the movies. But all I had were buttons and levers like a pinball machine, and a stupid voice telling me what I was doing wrong. The winning score here was my life.

The ground was starting to take shape now. I could see landmarks. The rear monitor showed smoke rolling off my hull, and I could smell burning insulation. Something told me that the lower decks were probably on fire, and that meant what was left of engineering was too; so my time in control was rapidly dwindling.

I watched what I guessed was the East Coast going by on the monitor, and then a couple of big cities. I judged I was traveling roughly in a southwesterly direction. My speed had slowed a lot, but I was still moving faster than any plane. I left whatever pursuit planes they launched far in the distance.

I crossed a large ribbon of water and figured it was the Mississippi River. That meant I was closing in on my destination. I was trying for either the desert, where this whole thing started, or the gulf. Anywhere without people.

I hit the port thruster again, and the front came around just a bit before it died. Now all that was left were the uppers and landing thrusters. Kansas shot by below me, and I started to force the front down again to dump altitude; but as I did, my speed increased once more. Nothing left to do but ride it out and pick my spot.

The sand of the desert was beginning as I pushed the front down even more, and we—me and a screaming ship, that is—dropped to about fifty feet above the ground. We were still traveling faster than the speed of sound. I hit the thruster again, and it puffed out of existence. It was just me and the ship now. A rock from space and a rock head inside it.

Twenty-five feet, ten feet! Sand was blowing up over the front of the saucer now, and the fires had reached the upper deck. The bridge was starting to fill with smoke. I squeezed my eyes tight and braced my feet. It could only be seconds now!

CHAPTER 24

The shuttle had been nowhere close to being as fast as the larger ship, but Kate at the controls did her best to try and keep Rick in sight. Her father was pacing in the small bit of room behind her and yelling out maneuvers for Rick to try. Unfortunately, he couldn't hear him. "Dad, sit down before you give yourself a heart attack! Rick knows what he's doing." Then under her breath, she said, "Or at least I hope he does."

The Professor came up and sat down beside her, turning his chair to face her. Laying his hand on her knee, he said, "Remember, Kate. If anybody can get out of this, he can."

Like the bigger craft, the ground sailed by under them, and they watched as the ship began to lose altitude as it started into the desert. It skimmed the top of the sand. The front caught and it rolled over and over. Smoke was streaming from the underside. Cracks began to appear in the dome as it was bashed against the ground with each roll.

It tumbled over a small rise and dropped out of sight. Then suddenly a flash of blinding light and a roar filled the desert. Smoke and flames leaped far into the sky beyond the rise.

Kate brought the small shuttle belly down onto the sand, and even before it stopped sliding, she was out and running towards the rise. As she reached the top, she had to turn her face away in horror. Below her was only fire and smoke. And parts of the saucer scattered for miles across the desert.

Her father came up beside her and took her in his arms. Kate buried her face in his shoulder and began to cry. There was nothing left to be said. No one could have survived that.

The Professor was holding Kate when suddenly his eyes got big and round. Not more than fifty feet away, a battered figure in a silver jumpsuit limped across the sand!

He pushed Kate gently away and turned her towards the limping figure. "Don't you think, Kate, maybe you should give him a hand?"

"What?" She dried her eyes and looked off where he pointed. In less than a breath, she was running across the sands, hitting Rick like a freight train, knocking him onto the sand.

* * * * *

I watched the dome crack and break over my head. It had been designed for the forces of deep space, but nothing like the punishment it was taking now. And as the chunks flew away, an idea began to form in my bird-like brain. If I could make my way to the edge on one of the rolls, I could use the force to get myself thrown free.

Timing was going to be everything. So I waited until the ship was in the back half of its roll and climbed from the seat, racing my way through the smoke to the edge of the dome just as the rear was starting to rise again. I waited until the front hit, and when it rolled, I leaped.

Even with the soft spot I landed in, I hit the sand like a rock, smacking down and knocking the breath from my lungs. A black cloud slid in to cover my eyes, and I began to die. Or at least that's what I thought. And because of the pain that was waiting for me seconds later when I came back, I wished I had. I came back just in time to watch the ship go up in flames.

As I lay there trying to learn to breathe again, I saw Kate run to the top of the rise and heard her scream. Then her father was there, holding her as she cried. I knew I couldn't let her cry. I never want to make her cry.

So with what little life I had left, I pulled myself to my feet, and on wobbly knees I limped across the sand. The Professor saw me first, then Kate. When she knocked me down, she did almost as much damage as the crash. But I wasn't complaining. She was covering my beat-up face with kisses so fast I didn't have time to kiss her back. I just closed my eyes and lay back to enjoy.

Would you like to see your manuscript become a book?

If you are interested in becoming a PublishAmerica author, please submit your manuscript for possible publication to us at:

acquisitions@publishamerica.com

You may also mail in your manuscript to:

PublishAmerica
PO Box 151
Frederick, MD 21705

www.publishamerica.com

CPSIA information can be obtained at www.ICGtesting.com

228672LV00001B/17/P